Short Story International

SHORT STORY INTERNATIONAL

Tales by the World's
Great Contemporary Writers
Presented Unabridged

All selections in
Short Story International
are reprinted full and
unabridged in the author's
own words. Nothing is
added, subtracted,
condensed or rewritten.

Editor
Sylvia Tankel

Associate Editor
Erik Sandberg-Diment

Contributing Editor
John Harr

Assistant Editors
Mildred Butterworth
Arlene Loveless
Kirsten Hammerle

Art Director
Mort Rubenstein

Drawings by
John Groth

Circulation Director
Nat Raboy

Production Director
Ludwig K. Marz

Business Manager
John O'Connor

Publisher
Sam Tankel

Volume 5; Number 25, April 1981.
Short Story International (USPS 375-970)
Copyright © by International Cultural
Exchange 1981. Printed in the U.S.A. All
rights reserved. Reproduction in whole or
in part prohibited. Second-class postage
paid at Great Neck, N.Y. 11022 and at
additional mailing offices. **Editorial
offices: P.O. Box 405, Great Neck,
N.Y. 11022.** Enclose stamped, self-
addressed envelope with previously
published stories submitted for possible
reprinting in *Short Story International*.
Please note *SSI* does not accept
unpublished original manuscripts. One
year (six issues) subscription for U.S.,
U.S. possessions $15, Canada $17, other
countries $20. Single copy price $2.95.
**For subscriptions and address
changes write to *Short Story
International*. 352 Evelyn Street,
Paramus, N.J. 07652.** *Short Story
International* is published bimonthly by
International Cultural Exchange, 6 Sheffield
Road, Great Neck, N.Y. 11021. Postmaster
please send Form 3579 to 352 Evelyn
Street, Paramus, N.J. 07652.

Note from the Editor

It seems every generation reinvents the wheel. And every generation rediscovers the vitality of the short story.

The printed short story had been run down by the television juggernaut in recent years. But like such short story heroines as Cinderella and the Adelaide of Damon Runyon's "Guys and Dolls," the short story has a lot of staying power. To paraphrase Mark Twain when he read his obituary: the reports of its demise were slightly exaggerated.

The world of the short story is without end. In *Short Story International* the entire spectrum of story-telling is represented—all corners of the world, all forms of subject, from wit to wisdom, from satire to sci-fi. Mystery and history, fantasy and quasi-documentary, motion and emotion—all are part of the world of the short story, and the world of *SSI*.

In this issue are the power, epiphany and the long reach of the short story. There is brisk satire . . . and delightful humor. There are stories focusing on the problems of the expatriate, of parents rigid in their ways, of the returned handicapped soldier, of the overly sensitive, of earthquakes, of love, of hope . . . of life.

Each issue brings its own mix. Our job is to present the work of talented contemporary writers from all over the globe. That is why we keep saying: *SSI* is a reflection of today's world; it is a chunk of contemporary history *and* a good read. We like to think the short story has found its hearth, its home, here at *SSI*.

Copyrights and acknowledgments

We wish to express deep thanks to the authors, publishers, translators and literary agents for their permission to reprint the stories in this issue.

"The Butterfly" (La mariposa) by Marco Denevi first appeared in Ficción (No. 29). Translation by Gregory Woodruff. Copyright © 1961 Marco Denevi. "Mrs. Dultz—Traveler" by Judith Womersley was originally broadcast on radio in Victoria. Copyright 1976 Judith Womersley. "The Key to My Heart" from Selected Stories by V.S. Pritchett. Published by Random House. Copyright © 1978 V.S. Pritchett. Reprinted by permission of Literistic, Ltd. and Chatto & Windus Ltd. "All Right Son, You Just Go By the Book" by Sandra Woolley first appeared in The Evening News. Copyright © 1977 Sandra Woolley. "Saree of the Gods" by G.S. Sharat Chandra first appeared in Female, Singapore. Copyright G.S. Sharat Chandra. "The Return" originally appeared in Escape for Short Distances by Shammai Golan. Copyright © 1976 Shammai Golan. Translated by Richard Flantz. "Caught in the Middle" by Shahnon Ahmad first appeared in Modern Malaysian Stories. Copyright © 1977 Shahnon Ahmad. Translation by Dr. Barclay M. Newman. Published by Dewan Bahasa dan Pustaka. "The Hunted Hare" by Edith Campion originally appeared in Landfall 129. Copyright © 1979 Edith Campion. "The Child" by Cora Sandel. Translation by Lydia Cranfield. Reprinted by permission of Erik Jonsson. Copyright © Erik Jonsson. "The Codger" from Nie strzelaj do organisty by Maria Nurowska. English translation by Edward Rothert first appeared in Polish Perspectives, 1976. Copyright Maria Nurowska. Reprinted by permission of the author and Authors' Agency Ltd. "The Man in the Dust" by Jane Meiring first appeared in Blackwood's Magazine. Reprinted by permission of the author and editor of Blackwood's Magazine. "Spring Will Come" by Fred D. Berkebile first appeared in Woman's Day. Copyright © Fred D. Berkebile. "Richter 10" by L.A.P. Moore originally appeared in Cavalier. Copyright © 1976 L.A.P. Moore. "Dona Lula and the Quetzal" by Yuri Kossatch first appeared in The Ukrainian-American, (now Monthly English Edition of the Ukrainian News). Copyright © 1977 Yuri Kossatch. "A Trip Into Life" by Meša Selimović. Copyright Meša Selimović. Translation by Rosario Glasnovic.

Photo credits: V.S. Pritchett by Jill Krementz. Edith Campion by John Ashton. L.A.P. Moore by Robert W. Free, Jr. Yuri Kossatch sketch by Maya Zatenetska.

Table of Contents

"One generation more,
and the traditions were forgotten
entirely."

The Butterfly

BY MARCO DENEVI

Lustrous social satire.

AS opposed to the locusts (who, as a result of knowing nothing
except how to sing, fell into a state of shocking decadence and
became extinct), the ants formed from their very beginnings a pro-
gressive society. And since progress, once in motion, never stops,
the ants one day achieved perfection.

To this perfection the discovery of synthetic vegetation is supposed to have contributed a great deal. The workers (dumb, blind,
deaf, sterile, and suitably brain-washed), after a special training
program, were shut up in dim, solitary cells where, regurgitating a
brew of unhatched larvae, they secreted a substance which had the
color, the taste, and all the other properties of natural vegetation, but
with the advantage that it was not necessary to leave the anthill to
harvest it. A whole series of anti-progressive factors was thus elim-
inated at one stroke: the ants were no longer dependent on the
caprices of nature, they were—as they were beginning to put it—

self-sufficient.

But if it was no longer necessary to leave the anthills, it was necessary to enlarge them, because the ant population tends to increase constantly. Underground tunnels and galleries branched out unceasingly. Rooms multiplied. Endless corridors connected endless storehouses. Until finally, meeting, separating, meeting again, all the anthills ended by merging into one single giant anthill, henceforth called the Great Anthill, under the rule of a single ant, known as the Great Ant. This did not come to pass without some difficulty (without a struggle). But in the end the Great Ant, solidly established, unified all the anthills by law, just as successive expansions had unified them in fact; frontiers were wiped out, nationalities were abolished, and Peace and Order reigned forever.

Did I say that the ants no longer needed to leave the Great Anthill? Nor could they, even had they wished to. For the Great Ant—and this was evidence of her sagacity and prudence—ordered the exits to be sealed up with stone and mortar, so that no one (or nothing, short of a catastrophic earthquake or the end of the world) might come to trouble the peace and order of her domain. With the result that, after two or three generations had passed, the ants fell (inevitably, of course) into the logical error of identifying the whole vast universe with the Great Anthill.

It is true that, in the early days, survivors of the Old Guard could still recall, though more and more dimly (because the ant has rather a feeble memory), a time when they had had to leave the anthill to find provender. Once started on these reminiscences, they would get carried away and never finish.

"Young people," they would say, raising a forefinger, "life was not easy in those days. It was a struggle, a hard struggle. But nobody complained."

The youngsters knew this was the inevitable prelude to an account of some great deed, for instance the discovery of a dead beetle, and the fabulous journey (parts of the story verged on frenzy and madness) of the four heroes who dragged the giant corpse for an entire day along a route which exposed them to unknown perils at every turn, until they reached the anthill at last. At the gates they fell dead of exhaustion, all but the chief (who, however, later committed suicide, as a point of honor).

And the ancients would conclude, with a touch of resentment (or perhaps of nostalgia), "Boys, that was real work."

But the old ones died, and the following generations, who had never left the extensive confines of the Great Anthill, began to refer to these tales as to some epic of a barbarous and remote age, though with some basis in historic fact; presently they thought of them as a body of fantastic legends, and at last as a jumble of foolish superstitions. And ended by finding them completely unintelligible, and dismissing them. By this time nobody understood what was meant by "rain," "summer" or "beetle." One generation more, and the traditions were forgotten entirely. The ants talked of nothing but techniques of brain-washing, or of hibernation as a method of preserving unhatched larvae, or the role of cybernetics in the large-scale production of synthetic vegetation, and other interesting subjects of the kind. If they still used a few words from the old language, it was in a purely metaphorical sense, as when, for instance, they would say "day" to refer to a certain intensity of the artificial light whose pallid rays illuminated the vaults and corridors of the Great Anthill. In short, after four generations the ants had shaken off even the memory of the past, which is the greatest known obstacle in the march of progress.

But one day in the Age of the Great Anthill, something unusual occurred.

It happened—how, we shall never know—that an ant got lost in a maze of galleries which had long since been abandoned. In vain she searched for a trail which would lead her back. All around her was darkness and silence. She came to a tunnel in ruins, at the end of which she thought she could make out a dim dying light. Terror-stricken though she was (for an ant can endure anything except being alone), she managed to advance cautiously toward this faint gleam. A closer approach confirmed the fact that it was indeed an exit, and that the light came from outside. They must have forgotten to seal it up at the time the Great Anthill was founded. Or perhaps the rain, or earth movement, or the mere passage of time had caused it to fall in. We do not know. All we know is that the ant gazed at the open door in wonder, and then, with her heart throbbing, disappeared through it.

And found herself outside the Great Anthill.

She took a few steps, like a sleepwalker.

She looked around.

What she saw she was never able to describe. She did not know what a garden was, what night was, or the moon, or water, or a rose. But now she beheld a garden, asleep or in a trance under the moonlight. She saw the moon, like a Great Ant, only round and white, and the stars trailing across the sky like a stream of ants in a daze. She saw the wash of grass, fretting beneath the weight of the dew. She saw a rose, like a censer shedding in the dark its heavy, voluptuous perfume. She saw the graveled path, the pergola, the statue. She saw, beyond, the still froth of foliage, with enameled goldfish weaving in and out. And, hardly daring to trust her senses, she heard the song of the crickets.

The ant stood still, rapt. But presently she started to run. She leaped over the pebbles, she dived into the grass, she ran here and there, this way and that. As though she had gone crazy.

"Oh my God," she sobbed, "how beautiful it all is!"

She wanted to see, see more, see everything, feel it, sense it, breathe it in, drink it down. The scents intoxicated her. The music of the night plunged her into a delirium sweeter than dreams. She listened to the song of the crickets, and her eyes filled with tears. Profound tremors shook her body. There was a pounding in her chest. She felt as though she was dying.

And over and over she kept saying: "How beautiful it all is, how beautiful!"

She was not merely frolicking in the grass by this time. She was leaping, and each leap was wilder, more daring than the one before. (How was she able, tiny as she was, with her little black feet, how was she able to leap like that? She neither knew nor cared.) She was swinging on a clump of azaleas, and a second later she was falling, panting and spent, at the foot of the statue.

Suddenly she thought of her sisters, and was choked by a fit of laughing. Poor things, living down there in those horrid underground caves, feeding on that cold bottled pap. She would go to them, she would spread the glad tidings, tell them what she had seen, and the ants would come out, they would leave the Great Anthill forever (whose idea was it, anyway, that they should be shut up in an anthill), and they would live, from today on, under that Great Ant, white and round, who led her flocks to graze on the vast luminous plain.

She leaped an enormous leap, searched for the entrance to the anthill, failed to find it, found it at last, entered with some difficulty (but why with difficulty, if when she had passed through before the gate had struck her as being monumental?), raced once more through the deserted corridors; she could barely see; the smell of damp earth, of confinement, sickened her; her head swam; there was no air to breathe; now she really felt as though she were near death; faint, dizzy, wounded, she still kept moving, dragging herself along, falling at every step, getting up, falling again; she still kept crawling, crawling, crawling until she could go no further. At this moment she heard voices.

A group of ants was having a heated discussion about the most recent discoveries in the field of industrial automation. They heard a noise behind them, and turned round. Panic seized them.

For there, before their eyes, a monster had appeared, a creature out of nightmare, an abomination. It was not black, as they were, but golden, with a body as long as four ants put together. Extraordinary antennae quivered above its misshapen head. And (this was the crowning horror) from its back four membranes sprouted, and these membranes were dazzling, iridescent, speckled, yellow veined with blue, streaked with purple. In short, the hues of madness.

The ants did not hesitate. They threw themselves upon the monster and killed it.

Marco Denevi was born in 1922 in Sáenz Peña, where he still lives. His short stories and novels are highly successful; several have been filmed. Mr. Denevi is also an award-winning playwright. The story translation is by Gregory Woodruff.

"Like an ancient prow she sat up front,
missing no rock or escarpment of each small
island as it passed . . ."

Mrs. Dultz—Traveler

BY JUDITH WOMERSLEY

A gung-ho, inexperienced traveler.

"DULTZ," she would say. "Mrs. Clara Dultz. D-U-L-T-Z. Dultz." She seemed to have a desperate desire for the disinterested and dour Greeks running the hotel in Omia Square to remember her name. Through that one sensed she felt a bit safer, so that if she fell ill or rang down from her room, they would know who she was.

There was in fact no need for her to worry. Everyone knew Mrs. Dultz. Her voice, loud, clear and slightly whiny, preceded her down corridors in the hotel, and floated backwards down the alleys of the Flea Market as she bargained indefatigably for a copper jug or a new suitcase to house her myriad souvenirs. Toiling up the steps to the Parthenon, in the blazing white-dusted noon, or in the smooth purple night, there would be Mrs. Dultz. Talking to a Greek priest in his long, black, dusty gown and stiff pillbox hat, Mrs. Dultz could be heard earnestly asking the history of this famous place.

"It was marvelous," she would confide that night in the foyer of the hotel, where she invariably sat after her early dinner, "so old, but of course it was a pity they didn't smooth the path up to it. Not touch the building itself of course, that was historic, but just build a nice, open area in front, where you could walk without tripping over all those old stones and ruts. My Lordy, I even had my photo taken sitting in the center seat, you know, in the Theatre of Dionysos. Wait till they see that back in Leongatha."

She was determined to see everything, Mrs. Dultz. At dinner in the Plaka, the very old, hilly part of Athens, where the cats wound themselves thinly round casually fallen columns of some disregarded ancient building, Mrs. Dultz would be seen, perching precariously on a rickety chair outside the rubble filled surrounds of a sparse and gray restaurant, determinedly finishing a plate of moussaka.

"So greasy this food," she would confide in what she thought was an undertone, with a trail of tomato colored oil running down her chin, "bad for their livers in this heat. Notice how yellow their skins are. Everything with too much oil on it, even the salad."

She would confide that she had eaten at the hotel earlier, at seven, the earliest she could get a meal, but that someone had told her about the little restaurants in the Plaka and she wanted to try true Greek food for herself.

"Delicious," she would say to the Greek boy when he took her plate, "dee-lic-ious," drawing out the word with the emphasis one would use to a half-wit. "Very nice."

With a heave she would be out of her chair and waddling down the rocky road towards her hotel, guide book in one hand and map of Athens in the other.

One day the hotel put up a notice about a tour of the Greek islands. Mrs. Dultz put her name down after some discussion with the hawk-eyed Greek at the desk, about the amount it cost in Australian dollars. "I'm prone to seasickness, but I'll take the risk," she said.

The hotel guests duly assembled early the next morning inside the bus that was to take them to Piraeus for the boat to the islands. Mrs. Dultz, of course, was in a front seat. The ride through Athens was punctuated by stops at several other hotels to collect tourists, and by a lengthy visit by the bus driver to an apartment building, possibly for breakfast. Mrs. Dultz became restless. "Where is the man? We were told to be ready at eight o'clock, and now here it is a quarter past nine. This bus is like an oven."

Mrs. Dultz had dressed in her own way for the heat. She wore, as she almost invariably did, white slacks, with a shirt top over it, and a chain belt round her middle. It would be wrong to say waist, because she had none. She was stiffly corseted from the thighs to just under the bust, so that she looked like a stout cracker, tied only at one end. Hung around her were various pieces of jewelry, all of which jangled as she moved. Her drop earrings seemed almost to sweep her shoulders, and among other bracelets on her arms was one loosely hung with charms that she would impatiently shake up her arm, only to have it fall down again in a second. On her head, in deference to the fierce Greek sun, was an extraordinary hat, a sort of pillbox, but softened all round by layers of pastel colored tulle in loops, which presumably were meant to extend out enough around her face to protect her from sunburn.

Eventually the driver returned without a word, and the bus lumbered through the city to Piraeus, with its bright orange and blue boats moored to the jetty, and white, square apartment buildings layered up the hill behind, like Biblical buildings of plaster of Paris, in a Sunday school diorama.

The tourists were handed on to the boat by seamen who seemed a little softer of face than the taciturn city Greeks, and with the seasoned ease of all tourists, proceeded to arrange themselves and their belongings comfortably around the decks, as if in their own backyards. Mrs. Dultz sat up front, somewhat jammed into a small deck chair, sternly surveying the blameless and ordinary sea through binoculars slung around her neck.

The day was very hot and the sea dazzlingly bright, and before long several of the older passengers had gone inside to nod on the fitted lounges under the windows, jerking their heads up guiltily from time to time, as they realized that they were missing part of what they had paid for. Not so Mrs. Dultz. Like an ancient prow she sat up front, missing no rock or escarpment of each small island as it passed, occasionally raking the seas with her binoculars, leaving her post only for the excellent lunch provided in the ship's lounge at one o'clock.

The boat docked at Hydra soon after lunch and the passengers were left to wander at will along the sea front tucked down under the bare, powdery hills, where a cluster of houses meandered up to a line of cypresses. Along the waterfront were innumerable little shops shaking themselves out of their afternoon stupor with a rattle of blinds, for the untimely arrival of tourists who would finger and compare and try to calculate drachmas into dollars and deutsch marks, and in the end perhaps make missing siesta worthwhile.

Mrs. Dultz was everywhere. She particularly wanted a little white marble replica of the Parthenon which she had seen in several shops in Athens, but which she thought she might buy cheaper on Hydra. "No, too much," she could be heard saying slowly and loudly, "too much. I buy when you lower price. I no pay that much." The shopkeepers hunched their shoulders and spread their hands in a desultory shrug. They did not even bother to argue. They had seen many Mrs. Dultzs and the tourist boats came every day.

When the boat siren sounded, warning passengers to board, they straggled along the quay and up the gangway, tired, but for the most part triumphant. Mrs. Dultz was positively radiant. "I got it, Mrs. Linden," she told a fellow passenger. "I just bargained and wouldn't give up and eventually he knew I wouldn't pay his price and he gave in." She had her marble Parthenon, and a woven shoulder bag for her niece, and an ashtray dipped in gold paint with a picture of the Acropolis in the middle and a teaspoon with the Greek flag on one end. She had had a drink of campari and soda at one cafe and a bacclava at another. "Pretty little place," she said at large, "small though. Cut off really, except for the tourists. They must enjoy the boats coming."

On the trip home it was discovered that unbeknown to most passengers, the ship's photographer had taken a picture of everyone as they descended the gangway onto the waterfront. They were clipped up in the closed foredeck of the ship. Mrs. Dultz bought three copies of herself. "It's not every day I get my photo taken in Greece," she said, "and my sister and my married niece in Wagga will want one."

Back over the sea, deepened and stilled as the darkness settled like a soft cloak over the decks, the passengers were quieter, tired and stiffening with sunburn, and still from time to time examining their purchases. By the time the boat slid into place at Piraeus, it was quite dark, except for pricks of light, like braille, from the cafes along the waterfront and the houses up the hill.

Three buses were waiting to take the tourists back to their various hotels. Mrs. Dultz got into the second and the trip back to Athens began. It was a long trip and dark, and she could recognize no one from her hotel in the bus.

"Oh driver," she called from her seat in the middle of the bus, "you will stop at the Odio, won't you? I don't know where it is, but you must know it. Odio. O-D-I-O. Odio." The driver answered not a word. Maybe he didn't speak English, or more likely he simply couldn't be bothered answering this lady with the whiny voice, which was starting to sharpen with panic. Other passengers were let out from time to time at the Metropole or the Bacchus, and each time the voice of Mrs. Dultz came plaintively from the middle of the bus, with a different emphasis. "Odio. O-dio. Od-io. Odi-o." Not once did the driver answer her, nor, from some sort of communal embarrassment at her rising panic, did any of the other passengers reassure her. "Odio, driver. Can you hear me? O-dio." But he remained silent, his sandaled feet stretched out carelessly on the accelerator, in silent contempt for this woman who might be a rich foreigner, but for the moment was at his mercy.

Mrs. Dultz moved up the front to a seat vacated by one of the exiting passengers, the better to look for landmarks. "Odio, driver. Can you hear me? Odio. I can't remember the address but you must know it. O-dio. Odio. Oh my God, will I never get out of here. Odi-o."

More black city streets, filled with strangers, more large squares she had never seen before, and the bus filled with foreigners. "O-dio," she said plaintively, with wavering conviction, "Odio."

"Odio," announced the driver, bringing the bus to a halt. "Odio up there. Up there."

"Thank God," said Mrs. Dultz, "I thought I'd never get there. I thought we must have missed it. Odio. Thank God," and she heaved herself off the bus with damp and breathless relief and waddled up the street to where the neon sign flashed a reassuring wink to her and the flapping canopy a friendly wave.

Clara Dultz. Ludicrous old lady and intrepid traveler. She was old, she was silly, she was tasteless and she was invariably unwittingly

19

rude. But with no foreign language, no traveling companion except her guide books and her tourist maps, she had somehow got herself across the sea to a Europe as incomprehensible to her as the planet Venus, and just as remote. In unsuitable clothing, without a friend, constantly bewildered and endlessly overcharged, hot, sweating and filled with strange food, Clara Dultz battled on, the cities of Europe passing her in a bewildering parade of brass Eiffel Towers and marble Parthenons and plaster Towers of London. She somehow got herself on to the right train, and if she missed a trip through a misreading of the strange European way of expressing time, she undaunted would be there next day. Bull fights in Spain, beerhalls in Munich, the Tivoli Gardens in Copenhagen, Clara Dultz saw them all. She was often frightened, seldom at ease, constantly exhausted, but this was the only time she would ever have such a trip and nothing was to be missed. Her enthusiasm was unbounded, her interest indefatigable, her energy renewed each night for the challenges of the next day. She was Clara Dultz, widow from Leongatha and Boadicea, in corsets. She was a stout and sweating Joan of Arc in bangles. Her days were made up of seeking after monuments, and terror at losing her way. Of looking in museum cases and worrying about her hotel bill. Of standing solemnly before pictures in some damp and ancient church, with her mind fixed firmly on the next day's schedule. Clara Dultz grew tall as she waddled up that strange Greek street towards her Holy Grail of the Odio.

Judith Womersley is an established short story writer and poet in Australia, with work published in national dailies, literary magazines and anthologies. Several of her short stories have been broadcast on radio. Married, with three children, Mrs. Womersley also teaches in Melbourne.

"Every shopkeeper, my father used to say, woke up in the early hours of the morning thinking of how much she owed him, and dreaming of her fortune."

The Key to My Heart

BY V.S. PRITCHETT

A good-looking young man tries to collect a sizeable debt from a lady.

WHEN Father dropped dead and Mother and I were left to run the business on our own, I was twenty-four years old. It was the principal bakery in our town, a good little business, and Father had built it up from nothing. Father used to wink at me when Mother talked about their "first wedding." "How many times have you been married? Who was it that time?" he used to say to her. She was speaking of the time they first ventured out of the bakery into catering for weddings and local dances. For a long time, when I was a child, we lived over the shop; then Mother made Father take a house down the street. Later still, we opened a café next door but two to the shop, and our idea was to buy up the two little places in between. But something went wrong in the last years of Father's life. Working at night in the heat and getting up at the wrong time of day disorganized him. And then the weddings were his downfall. There is always champagne left over at weddings, and Father got to like it and live on it. And then brandy followed. When Mr. Pickering, the solicitor, went into the will and the accounts, there was muddle everywhere, and bills we had never heard of came in.

"Father kept it all in his head," Mother said, very proud of him for that. Mr. Pickering and I had to sort it all out, and one of the things we discovered was that what we owed was nothing to what people owed us. Mother used to serve in the shop and do the books. She did it, we used to say, for the sake of the gossip—to daydream about why the schoolmistress ordered crumpets only on Thursdays, or guessing, if someone ordered more of this kind of cake or that, who was going to eat it with them. She was generally right, and she knew more about what was going on in the town than anyone else. As long as the daily and weekly customers paid their books, she didn't bother; she hated sending bills, and she was more pleased than upset when Mr. Pickering told her there was a good six hundred pounds owing by people who either hadn't been asked to pay or who were simply not troubling themselves. In a small business, this was a lot of money. It was the rich and the big pots in the county who were the worst of these debtors. Dad and Mother never minded being owed by the rich. They had both grown up in the days when you were afraid of offending people, and to hear my mother talk you would have thought that by asking the well-off to fork out you were going to kill the goose that lays the golden egg, knock the bottom out of society, and let a Labor government in.

"Think of what they have to pay in taxes," she would say, pitying them. "And the death duties!" And when I did what Mr. Pickering said, and sent out accounts to these people, saying politely that it had no doubt been overlooked, Mother looked mournful and said getting a commission in the Army had turned my head. The money came in, of course. When Colonel Williams paid up and didn't dispute it, Mother looked at his check as if it were an insult from the old gentleman and, in fact, "lost" it in her apron pocket for a week. Lady Littlebank complained, but she paid all the same. A few did not answer, but when I called at their houses they paid at once. Though the look on Mother's face was as much as to say I was a son ruining her lifework and destroying her chances of holding her head up in society. At the end of two or three months there was only one large

account outstanding—a Mrs. Brackett's. Mrs. Brackett did not answer, and you can guess Mother made the most of this. Mother
spoke highly of Mrs. Brackett, said she was "such a lady," "came of
a wonderful family," and once even praised her clothes. She was the
richest woman in the county, and young. She became my mother's
ideal.

Mrs. Brackett was married to a pilot and racing motorist known in
the town as Noisy Brackett; it was she, as my mother said, nodding
her head up and down, who "had the money." Noisy was given a
couple of cars and his pocket money, but, having done that, Mrs.
Brackett paid as little as she could, as slowly as she could, to
everyone else. When I talked about her account to other shopkeepers in the town, they put on their glasses, had a look at their
books, sniffed, and said nothing. Every shopkeeper, my father used
to say, woke up in the early hours of the morning thinking of how
much she owed him, and dreaming of her fortune. You can work out
how long her bill with us had run on when I say it was nearly two
hundred and thirty pounds. The exact sum was two hundred and
twenty-eight pounds fourteen and fourpence. I shall always remember it.

The first time I made out Mrs. Brackett's bill, I gave it to Noisy. He
often came into the café to flirt with the girls, or to our shop to see
Mother and get her to cash checks for him. He was a thin little man,
straight as a stick and looked as brittle, and covered (they said) with
scars and wounds from his crashes. He had the curly shining black
hair of a sick gypsy, and the lines of a charmer all over his face. His
smiles quickly ended in a sudden, stern twitching of his left cheek and
eye, like the crack of a whip, which delighted the women. He was a
dandy, and from Mother he had the highest praise she could give to
any man. He was, she said, "snobby."

When I gave Noisy our bill, he handed it back to me at once. "Be a
sweetie-pie," he said, "and keep it under your hat until the day after
tomorrow. Tomorrow's my payday, and I don't want the Fairy
Queen to get her mind taken off it—d'you follow? Good! Fine!
Splendid fellow! Bang on!" And, with a twitch, he was back in his
long white Bentley. "Bring it yourself," he said, looking me up and
down. I am a very tall man, and little Noisy had a long way to look.

"It'll do the trick."

Noisy did not hide his dependence on his wife. Everyone except the local gentry liked him.

So on the Thursday, when the shop was closed and I could leave the café to the waitresses—a good pair of girls, and Rosie, the dark one, very pretty—I took the station wagon and drove up to Heading Mount, four miles out of the town. It was June; they were getting the hay in. The land in the valley fetches its price—you wouldn't believe it if I told you what a farm fetches there. Higher up, the land is poor, where the oak woods begin, and all that stretch that belonged to old Mr. Lucas, Mrs. Brackett's father, who had made a fortune out of machine tools. The estate was broken up when he died. I came out of the oak woods and turned into the drive, which winds between low stone walls and tall rhododendron bushes, so that it is like a damp, dark sunken lane, and very narrow. Couples often walked up on Sundays in June to see the show of rhododendrons on the slopes at Heading; the bushes were in flower as I drove by. I was speeding to the sharp turn at the end of the drive, before you come to the house, when I had to brake suddenly. Mrs. Bracket's gray Bentley was drawn broadside across it, blocking the drive completely. I ought to have seen this was a bad omen.

To leave a car like that, anywhere, was typical of Mrs. Brackett. If there was a traffic jam in the town, or if someone couldn't get into the market, nine times out of ten Mrs. Brackett's car was the cause. She just stepped out of it wherever it was, as if she were dropping her coat off for someone else to pick up. The police did nothing. As she got back in, she would smile at them, raise one eyebrow, wag her hips, and let them see as much of her legs as she thought fit for the hour of the day, and drive off with a small wave of her hand that made them swell with apologies and blow up someone else. Sometimes she went green with a rage that was terrifying coming from so small a person.

As I walked across the lawn, I realized I had missed the back lane to the house, and that I ought to have driven along a wire-fenced road across the fields to the farm and the kitchen, where the housekeeper lived. But I had not been up there for several years, and had forgotten it. As I walked towards the white front door, I kicked a woman's shoe—a shoe for a very small foot. I picked it up. I was a few yards from the door when Mrs. Brackett marched out, stopped on the steps, and then, as sharp as a sergeant, shouted, "Jimmy!" She was looking up at the sky, as though she expected to bring her husband down out of it.

She was barefooted, wearing a blue-and-white checked shirt and dusty jeans, and her short fair hair untidy, and she was making an ugly mouth, like a boy's, on her pretty face. I was holding out the shoe as I went forward. There was no answer to her shout. Then she saw me and stared at the shoe.

"Who are you? What are you doing with that?" she asked. "Put it down."

But before I could answer, from the other side of the buildings there was the sound of a car starting and driving off on the back road. Mrs. Brackett heard this. She turned and marched into the house again, but in a few seconds she returned, running past me across the lawn. She jumped into her car, backed—and then she saw mine blocking the drive. She sounded her horn, again and again. A dog barked, and she jumped out and bawled at me. "You bloody fool!" she shouted. "Get that van of yours out of the way!"

The language that came out of her small mouth was like what you hear in the cattle market on Fridays. I slowly went up and got into my van. I could hear her swearing and the other car tearing off; already it must have turned into the main road. I got into mine, and there we sat, face to face, scowling at each other through our windscreens. I reversed down the long, winding drive, very fast, keeping one eye on her all the time, and turned sharply off the road at the entrance. I don't mind saying I was showing off. I can reverse a car at speed and put it anywhere to within an inch of where I want to. I saw her face change as she came on, for in her temper she was coming fast down the drive straight at me, radiator to radiator. At the end, she gave one glance of surprise at me, and I think held back a word she had ready as she drove past. At any rate, her mouth was open. Half a dozen cows started from under the trees and went trotting round the field in panic as she went, and the rooks came out of the elms like bits of black paper.

By bad luck, you see, I had arrived in the middle of one of the regular Brackett rows. They were famous in the neighborhood. The Bracketts chased each other round the house, things came out of windows—clothes, boots, anything. Our roundsman said he had once seen a portable radio, playing full on, come flying out, and that it had fallen, still playing, in the roses. Servants came down to the town and said they had had enough of it. Money was usually at the bottom of the trouble. There was a tale going round that when a village girl who worked there got married, Mrs. Brackett gave her a three-shilling alarm clock for a wedding present.

The rows always went the same way. A car would race out of the drive with Noisy in it, and five minutes later Mrs. Brackett would be in her car chasing him, and no one was safe on the roads for twenty miles around. Sometimes it might end quietly in a country pub, with Mrs. Brackett in one bar and Noisy in the other, white-faced and playing hymns on the piano to mock her until she gave in. Other times, it might go on through the night. Noisy, who raced cars, was the better driver, but she was wilder. She would do anything—she once cut through the footpath of the cemetery to catch him on the other side. She sometimes caught him, but more than once her meanness about money would leave her standing. There would be a telephone call to Brigg's garage: Mrs. Brackett had run out of petrol. She was too mean ever to have much more than a gallon in the tank.

"Bless her," Noisy used to say if anyone mentioned these chases to him. "I always rely on the Fairy Queen to run out of gas."

Noisy was a woman-hater. His trouble was his habit of saying "Bless you" to the whole female sex.

"Well, I hope you're satisfied," my mother said when I got home. I put Mrs. Brackett's shoe on the table.

"I've made some progress," I said.

My mother looked at the shoe for a long time. Now that I had got something out of Mrs. Brackett, Mother began to think a little less of her. "You'd think a woman with feet like that would dress better," she said.

But what annoyed me was that at some stage in the afternoon's chase Noisy had slipped in and got Mother to cash him a check for twenty pounds.

June is the busy time of the year for us. There are all the June weddings. Noisy and Mrs. Brackett must have settled down again somehow, because I saw them driving through the town once or twice. I said to myself, "You wait till the rush is over."

In July, I went up to the Bracketts' house a second time. Rosie, the dark girl who works in our café, came with me, because she wanted to meet her aunt at the main-line station, three or four miles over the hill beyond Heading Mount, and I was taking her on there after I had spoken to Mrs. Brackett. I drove up to the house. The rhododendrons had died, and there were pods on them already going brown. The sun struck warm in front of the house. It was wonderfully quiet.

I left the girl in the car, reading a book, and was working out a sentence to say, when I saw Mrs. Brackett kneeling by a goldfish pond, at the far side of the great lawn. She turned and saw me. I did not know whether to go over the lawn to her or to wait where I was. I decided to go over, and she got up and walked to me. Mother was right about her clothes. This time she was wearing a gaudy tomato-colored cotton dress that looked like someone else's, and nothing on underneath it. I do not know why it was—whether it was because I was standing on the grass as she was walking over, whether it was my anxiety about how to begin the conversation, or whether it was because of her bare white arms, the dawdling manner of her walk, and the inquisitiveness of her eyes—but I thought I was going to faint. When she was two yards away, my heart jumped, my throat closed, and my head was swimming. Although I had often seen her driving through the town, and though I remembered our last meeting all too well, I had never really looked at her before. She stopped, but I had the feeling that she had not stopped, but was invisibly walking on until she walked clean through me. My arms went weak. She was amused by the effect she had on me.

"I know who you are," she said. "You are Mr. Fraser's son. Do you want to speak to me?"

I did, but I couldn't. I forgot all the sentences I had prepared. "I've come about our check," I said at last. I shouted it. Mrs. Brackett was as startled by my shout as I was. She blushed at the loudness and shock of it—not a light blush but a dark, red, flooding blush on her face and her neck that confused her and made her lower her head like a child caught stealing. She put her hands behind her back like a child. I blushed, too. She walked up and down a yard or two, her head still down, thinking. Then she walked away to the house.

"You'd better come inside," she called back in an offhand way.

You could have put our house into the hall and sitting-room of Heading Mount. I had been in that room when I was a boy, helping the waitress when my father was there doing the catering for a party. I do not know what you'd have to pay for the furniture there— thousands, I suppose. She led me through the room to a smaller room beyond it, where there was a desk. I felt I was slowly walking miles. I have never seen such a mess of papers and letters. They were even spread on the carpet. She sat down at the desk.

"Can you see the bill?" she muttered, not looking at me and pointing to the floor.

"I've got it here," I said, taking the bill out of my pocket. She jerked her head. The flush had gone, and now she looked as keen as needles at me.

"Well, sit down," she said.

She took the bill from me and looked at it. Now I could see that her skin was not white but was really pale and clay-colored, with scores of little cracks in it, and that she was certainly nearer forty than thirty, as Mother always said.

"I've paid this," she said, giving the bill a mannish slap. "I pay every quarter."

"It has been running for three and a half years," I said, more at ease now.

"What?" she said. "Oh, well, I paid something, anyway. This isn't a bill. It's a statement."

"Yes," I said. "We have sent you the bills."

"Where's the date? This hasn't got any date on it."

I got up and pointed to the date.

"It ought to be at the top," she said.

My giddiness had gone. Noisy came into the room. "Hullo, Bob," he said. "I've just been talking to that beautiful thing you have got in the car." He always spoke in an alert, exhausted way about women, like someone at a shoot waiting for the birds to come over. "Have you seen Bob's girl, darling?" he said to her. "I've just offered her the key to my heart." And he lifted the silk scarf he was wearing in the neck of his canary-colored pullover, and there was a piece of string round his neck with a heavy old door key hanging from it. Noisy gave a twitch to one side of his face.

"Oh, God, that old gag," said Mrs. Brackett.

"Not appreciated, old boy," said Noisy to me.

"Irresistible," said Mrs. Brackett, with an ugly mouth. She turned and spoke to me again, but glanced shrewdly at Noisy as she did so. "Let me try this one on you," she said. "You've already got my husband's checks for this bill. I send him down to pay you, and he just cashes them?"

"I'm afraid not, Mrs. Bracket," I said. "That wouldn't be possible."

"You can't get away with that one, my pet," said Noisy. "Are you ready to go out?" He looked at her dress, admiring her figure. "What a target, Bob," he said.

"I don't think we will ask Mr. Fraser's opinion," she said coldly, but very pleased. And she got up and started out of the room, with Noisy behind her.

"You had better send me the bills," she called back to me, turning round from the door.

I felt very, very tired. I left the house and slammed the car door when I got in. "Now she wants the damn bills," I said to Rosie as I drove her up to Tolton station. I did not speak to her the rest of the way. She irritated me, sitting here.

When I got home and told my mother, she was short with me. That was the way to lose customers, she said. I was ruining all the work she and Dad had put into the business. I said if Mrs. Brackett wanted her bills she could come and get them herself. Mother was very shocked.

She let it go for a day or two, but she had to bring it up again. "What are you sulking about?" she said to me one afternoon. "You upset Rosie this morning. Have you done those bills for Mrs. Brackett yet?"

I made excuses, and got in the car and went over to the millers and to the people who make our boxes, to get away from the nagging. Once I was out of the town, in the open country, Mrs. Brackett seemed to be somewhere just ahead of me, round a corner, over a hill, beyond a wood. There she was, trying to make me forget she owed us two hundred and twenty-eight pounds fourteen and fourpence. The moment she was in my head, the money went out of it. When I got back, late in the evening, Mother was on to me again. Noisy had been in. She said he had been sent down by his wife to ask why I had not brought the bills.

"The poor Wing Commander," my mother said. "Another rumpus up there." (She always gave him his rank if there was a rumor of another quarrel at Heading.) "She never gives him any peace. He's just an errand boy. She does what she likes with him."

"He's been offering you the key to his heart, Mother," I said.

"I don't take any stock of him," Mother said. "Or that pansy sweetheart stuff. Dad was the one and only for me. I don't believe in second marriages. I've no time for jealous women; they're always up to something, like Mrs. Doubleday thinking I spoke to her husband in the bank and she was caught with the chemist, but you always think the Fairy Prince will turn up—it's natural."

It always took a little time getting at what was in Mother's mind, yet it was really simple. She was a good churchwoman, and she thought Noisy was not really married to Mrs. Brackett, because he had been divorced by his first wife. She did not blame Noisy for this—in fact, she admired it, in a romantic way—but she blamed Mrs. Brackett, because, by Mother's theories, Mrs. Brackett was still single. And Mother never knew whether to admire single women for holding out or to suspect them of being on the prowl. One thing she was certain of. "Money talks," she said. The thing that made Noisy respectable for her, and as good as being married in church, was that he had married Mrs. Brackett for her money.

She talked like this the night we sat up and did that month's bills, but the next day—and this was the trouble with Mother—it ended in a row. I sent the bills up to Mrs. Brackett by our delivery van.

"That is not the way to behave," Mother said. "You should have taken them yourself."

And before the day was out, Mother was in a temper again. Mrs. Brackett had spoken to her on the telephone and said she had been through the bills and that we had charged her for things she hadn't had, because she'd been in the South of France at the time.

"I told you to go," Mother said to me.

I was angry, too, at being called dishonest. I got out the van and said I was going up at once.

"Oh, that's how it is," said my mother, changing round again. "Her Ladyship snaps her fingers and you go up at once. She's got you running about for her like Noisy. If I ask you to do anything, you don't pay attention to me. But Mrs. Brackett—she's the Queen of England. Two of you running after her."

Mother was just like that with Father when he was alive. He took no notice. Neither did I. I went up to Heading. A maid let me in, and I sat there waiting in the drawing-room. I waited a long time, listening to the bees coming down the chimney, circling lower and lower and then roaring out into the room, like Noisy's car. I could hear Mrs. Brackett talking on the telephone in her study. I could hear now and then what she was saying. She was a great racing woman, and from words she said here and there I would say she was speaking to a bookmaker. One sentence I remember, because I think it had the name of a horse in it, and when I got back home later I looked up the racing news to see if I could find it. "Tray Pays On," she said. She came out into the room with the laughter of her telephone call still on her face. I was standing up, with our account book in my hand, and when she saw me the laughter went.

I was not afraid of her any more. "I hear there is some trouble about the bills," I said. "If you've got them, you can check them with the book. I've brought it."

Mrs. Brackett was a woman who watched people's faces. She put on her dutiful, serious, and obedient look, and led me again to the little room where the papers were. She sat down and I stood over her while we compared the bills and the book. I watched one by one, and she nodded and ticked the bills with a pencil. We checked for nearly half an hour. The only thing she said was in the middle of it—"You've got a double jointed thumb. So have I"—but she went right on.

"I can see what it is," I said at the end. "You've mistaken 1953 for '54."

She pushed the book away, and leaned back in the chair against my arm, which was resting on it.

"No, I haven't," she said, her small, unsmiling face looking up into mine. "I just wanted you to come up."

She gazed at me a long time. I thought of all the work Mother and I had done, and then that Mother was right about Mrs. Brackett. I took my hand from the chair and stepped back.

"I wanted to ask you one or two things," she said, confidingly, "about that property next to the shop. I'll be fair with you. I'm interested in it. Are you? All right, don't answer. I see you are."

My heart jumped. Ever since I could remember, Father and Mother had talked of buying this property. It was their daydream. They simply liked little bits of property everywhere, and now I wanted it so that we could join the shop and the café.

"I asked because . . ." She hesitated. "I'll be frank with you. The bank manager was talking about it to me today."

My fright died down. I didn't believe that the bank manager—he was Mr. Pickering's brother-in-law—would let my mother down and allow the property to go to Mrs. Brackett without giving us the offer first.

"We want it, of course," I said. And then I suspected this was one of her tricks. "That is why I have been getting our bills in," I said.

"Oh, I didn't think that was it," she said. "I thought you were getting married. My husband says you are engaged to the girl you brought up here. He said he thought you were. Has she any money?"

"Engaged!" I said. "I'm not. Who told him that?"

"Oh," she said, and then a thought must have struck her. I could read it at once. In our town, if you cough in the High Street the chemist up at the Town Hall has got a bottle of cough mixture wrapped up and waiting for you; news travels fast. She must have guessed that when Noisy came down dangling the key to his heart, he could have been round the corner all the time, seeing Rosie.

"I'm glad to hear you're not engaged," Mrs. Brackett said tenderly. "I like a man who works. You work like your father did—God, what an attractive man! You're like him. I'm not flattering you. I saw it when you came up the first time."

She asked me a lot of questions about the shop and who did the baking now. I told her I didn't do it and that I wanted to enlarge the restaurant. "The machine bakeries are getting more and more out into the country," I said. "And you've got to look out."

"I don't see why you shouldn't do catering for schools," she said. "And there's the Works." (Her father's main factory.) "Why don't you get hold of the catering there?"

"You can only do that if you have capital. We're not big enough," I said, laughing.

"How much do you want?" she said. "Two thousand? Three? I don't see why we couldn't do something."

The moment she said "we" I came to my senses. Here's a funny turnout, I thought. She won't pay her bills, but first she's after these shops, and now she's waving two thousand pounds in my face. Everyone in our town knew she was artful. I suppose she thought I was green.

"Not as much as two thousand," I said. "Just the bill," I said, nodding at it.

Mrs. Brackett smiled. "I like you. You're interested in money. Good. I'll settle it." And, taking her check book from the top of the desk, she put it in her drawer. "I never pay these accounts by check. I pay in cash. I'll get it tomorrow at the bank. I'll tell you what I'll do. You've got a shoe of mine. Bring it up tomorrow evening at, say, half past eight. I'll be back by then and you can have it." She paused, and then, getting up, added quickly, "Half tomorrow, half in October."

It was like dealing with the gypsies that come to your door.

"Now, Mrs. Brackett," I said. "I'd like all of it. Now." We stared at each other. It was like that moment months ago when she had driven at me in her car and I had reversed down the drive with one eye watching her and one on the road as I shot back. That was the time, I think, I first noticed her—when she opened her mouth to shout a word at me and then did not shout. I could have stayed like this, looking into her small, pretty, miser's blue eyes, at her determined head, her chopped-off fair hair, for half an hour. It was a struggle.

She was the first to speak, and that was a point gained to me. Her voice shook a little. "I don't keep that amount of money in the house," she said.

I knew that argument. Noisy said she always had two or three hundred pounds in the safe in the wall of her study, and whether this was so or not, I could not help glancing towards it.

"I don't like being dictated to," she said, catching my glance. "I have told you what I will do."

"I think you could manage it, Mrs. Brackett," I said.

I could see she was on the point of flying into one of her tempers, and as far as I was concerned (I don't know why), I hoped she would. Her rows with Noisy were so famous that I must have wanted to see one for myself. And I didn't see why she should get away with it. At the back of my mind, I thought of all the others down in the town and how they would look when I said I had got my money out of Mrs. Brackett.

Yet I wasn't really thinking about the money at all, at this moment. I was looking at her pretty shoulders.

But Mrs. Brackett did nót fly into a temper. She considered me, and then she spoke in a quiet voice that took me off my guard. "Actually," she said, lowering her eyes, "you haven't been coming up here after money at all, have you?"

"Well—" I began.

"Sh-h-h!" she said, jumping up from her chair and putting her hand on my mouth. "Why didn't you ring me and tell me you were coming? I am often alone."

She stepped to the door and bawled out, "Jimmy!" as if he were a long way off. He was—to my surprise, and even more to hers—very near.

"Yes, ducky?" Noisy called back from the hall.

"Damn," she said to me. "You must go." And, squeezing my hand, she went through the drawing-room into the hall.

"What time do we get back tomorrow evening?" she said boldly to Noisy. "Half past eight? Come at half past eight," she said, turning to me, for I had followed her. "I'll bring back the cash."

The sight of Noisy was a relief to me, and the sound of the word "cash" made Noisy brighten.

"Not lovely little bits of money!" he exclaimed.

"Not you," said Mrs. Brackett, glaring at him.

"How did you work it, old boy?" said Noisy later, giving me one of his most quizzical twitches as he walked with me to my van. When I drove off, I could see him still standing there, watching me out of sight.

I drove away very slowly. My mind was in confusion. About half a mile off, I stopped the car and lit a cigarette. All the tales I had heard about Mrs. Brackett came back into my mind. It was one thing to look at her, another thing to know about her. The one person I wished I had with me was Noisy. He seemed like a guarantor of safety, a protection. To have had my thoughts read like that by her filled me with fear.

I finished my cigarette. I decided not to go straight home, and I drove slowly all along the lower sides of the oak woods, so slowly and carelessly that I had to swerve to avoid oncoming cars. I was making, almost without knowing it, for the Green Man, at Mill Cross. There was a girl there I had spoken to once or twice. No one you would know. I went in and asked for a glass of beer. I hardly said a word to her, except about the weather, and then she left the bar to look after a baby in the kitchen at the back. That calmed me. I think the way she gave me my change brought me back to earth and made me feel free of Mrs. Brackett's spell. At any rate, I put the threepence in my pocket and swallowed my beer. I laughed at myself. Mrs. Brackett had gypped me again.

When I got home, it was late, and my mother was morose. She was wearing a black dress she often wore when she was alone, dressed up and ready to go out, yet not intending to, as if now that my father was dead she was free if someone would invite her. Her best handbag was beside her. She was often waiting like this, sitting on the sofa, doing nothing but listening to the clock tick, and perhaps getting up to give a touch to some flowers on the table and then sitting down again. Her first words shook me.

"Mrs. Brackett was down here looking for you," she said sharply. "I thought you were with her. She wants you to be sure to go up tomorrow evening to collect some money when she comes back from Tolton. Where have you been?"

"Let the old bitch post it or bring it in," I said.

Mother was horrified at the idea of Mrs. Brackett soiling her hands with money.

"You'll do as I tell you," she said. "You'll go up and get it. If you don't Noisy will get his hands on it first. You'd think a woman with all that money would go to a decent hairdresser. It's meanness, I suppose."

And then, of course, I saw I was making a lot of fuss about nothing. Noisy would be there when I went up to Heading. Good old Noisy, I thought; thank God for that. And he'll see I get the money, because she said it in front of him.

So the next evening I went. I put my car near the garage, and the first person I saw was Noisy, standing beside his own car. He had a suitcase in his hand. I went over to him.

"Fairy Queen's been at work," he said. He nodded at his tires. They were flat. "I'm doing some quick thinking."

At that moment, a top window of the house was opened and someone emptied a suitcase of clothes out of it, and then a shower of cigarettes came down.

"She's tidying," he said. "I've got a quarter of an hour to catch the London train. Be a sweetie-pie and run me over there."

I had arrived once more in the middle of one of the Brackett rows. Only this time Noisy was leaving it to me. That is how I felt about it. "Hop in," I said.

And when we were off and a mile from Heading, he sat up in the seat and looked round. "Nothing on our tail," he said.

"Have you ever heard of a horse called Tray?" I asked him. "Tray Pays something? Tray Pays On—that can't be it."

"Tray Pays On?" repeated Noisy. "Is it a French horse?"

"I don't know," I said.

"Bloody peasant? Could be," said Noisy. "Sounds a bit frog to me."

We got to Tolton station. Noisy was looking very white and set with hatred. Not until he was standing in the queue getting his ticket did it occur to me what Noisy was doing.

"The first time I've traveled by train for fifteen years," he called to me across from the queue. "Damned serious. You can tell her if you see her"—people stared—"the worm has turned. I'm packing it in for good."

And as he went off to the train, he called, "I suppose you are going back? No business of mine, but I'll give you a tip. If you do, you won't find anything in the kitty, Bob." He gave me his stare and his final twitch. It was like the crack of a shot. Bang on, as he would have said. A bull's-eye.

I walked slowly away as the London train puffed out. I took his advice. I did not go back to Heading.

There were rows and rows between the Bracketts, but there was none like this one. It was the last. The others were a chase. This was not. For only Mrs. Brackett was on the road that night. She was seen, we were told, in all the likely places. She had been a dozen times through the town. Soon after ten o'clock she was hooting outside our house. Mother peeped through the curtains, and I went out. Mrs. Brackett got out of her car and marched at me. "Where have you been?" she shouted. "Where is my husband?"

"I don't know," I said.

"Yes, you do," she said. "You took him to Tolton, they told me."

"I think he's gone to London," I said.

"Don't be a damn liar," she said. "How can he have? His car is up there."

"By train," I said.

"By train," she repeated. Her anger vanished. She looked at me with astonishment. The rich are very peculiar. Mrs. Brackett had forgotten people travel by train. I could see she was considering the startling fact. She was not a woman to waste time staying in one state of mind for long. Noisy used to say of her, "That little clock never stops ticking."

"I see," she said to me sarcastically, nodding out the words. "That's what you and Jimmy have been plotting." She gave a shake to her hair and held her chin up. "You've got your money and you don't care," she said.

"What money is that?" I said.

"What money!" she exclaimed sharply, going over each inch of my face. What she saw surprised her at first. Until then she had been fighting back, but now a sly look came to her; it grew into a smile; the smile got wider and wider, and then her eyes became two curved lines, like crow's wings in the sky, and she went into shouts of laughter. It sounded all down the empty street. She rocked with it.

"Oh, no!" she laughed. "Oh, no, that's too good! That's a winner.

He didn't give you a penny! He swiped the lot!"

And she looked up at the sky in admiration of that flying man. She was still grinning at me when she taunted breathlessly. "I mean to say—I mean to say—"

I let her run on.

"It was all or nothing with you, wasn't it?" she said. "And you get nothing, don't you?"

I am not sure what I did. I may have started to laugh it off and I may have made a step towards her. Whatever I did, she went hard and prim, and if ever a woman ended anything, she did then. She went over to the car, got in, and slammed the door.

"You backed the wrong horse when you backed Jimmy," she called out to me.

That was the last of her. No more Mrs. Brackett at the shop. "You won't hear another word from her," my mother said.

"What am I supposed to do—get her husband back?" I said.

By the end of the week, everyone in the town was laughing and winking at me.

"You did the trick, boy," the grocer said.

"You're a good-looking fellow, Bob," the ironmonger said.

"Quite a way with the girls," the butcher said. "Bob's deep."

For when Mrs. Brackett went home that night, she sat down and paid every penny she owed to every shopkeeper in the town. Paid everyone, I say. Bar me.

Born in 1900 in England, Sir V. S. Pritchett is a distinguished and versatile writer who is often referred to as the finest English writer alive. His work includes short stories, novels, literary criticism, biography, autobiography and books of travel. He received a knighthood in 1975. Sir Victor is a foreign honorary member of the American Academy of Arts and Letters and of the Academy of Arts and Sciences. He lives in London with his wife.

> "They were talking about me
> and some old folks home."

All Right Son,
You Just Go By the Book

BY SANDRA WOOLLEY

An unanticipated turn of events.

NOW as I always say—and it's true I'm sure—it's not a lot of fun getting old. But like most things it has its compensations.

People try to be very understanding. You can get away with murder. You know what I mean? Think about it. I've given it a lot of thought.

You see, in the main folk tend to treat an old 'un with a little more tolerance—patience if you like. They may mutter "Silly old fool!" behind your back. But deep down they know that all things being equal—they're going to get old, too.

Then *we* may act a little clumsy—or get a bit deaf. I mean, when you're pushing 80 like me, well, it's only to be expected.

Maybe you don't see it now—but you will when I've finished.

I'm luckier than most. Never had much but then I never really needed a lot. The old limbs may be weaker—but my ears and eyes are still good as new.

So you'll maybe understand how I felt when I heard our Pat and Eddie talking about "What's to become of dad?"

Well, it wasn't Pat so much as Eddie. I cannot deny that my son-in-law and myself have never had a lot of time for each other. You see, he married Pat against my wishes.

Just after their honeymoon I had cause to give him a hiding. That was after I discovered he'd blacked her eye. Perhaps I should have minded my own business. Anyway, after that we did have a kind of gentlemen's agreement. He kept his hands off her and I kept my hands off him.

But I'm getting off the point. I overheard the pair of them talking . . .

Now it must have been last Thursday because I'd been down for my pension, the weather was a bit sharp and on my way back I'd dropped into the Anglers for a nip—helps me breathing on a cold day, you see.

They were talking about me and some old folks home. I wasn't so much shocked as hurt—if you know what I mean.

After all, I'd given up the flat when my old lady passed on because Pat had said that it would be easier all round if I moved in with them.

I wasn't too happy at the time, mind. But she gave me a couple of rooms to myself—so it wasn't as if we were under each other's feet. In fact I'd thought everything was working out well. Just shows how wrong you can be.

I listened to them for a while and I could tell that my Pat was trying her best to talk him round to her way of thinking. But Eddie was having none of it. He was paying me off for that thumping all those years back.

I was impressed. I'd never known him work so hard and my little girl was definitely weakening. She never had been any match for him and his wiles.

There seemed little sense in bursting in and having an up-and-downer with them, so I slipped out of the back door and went down to Green Street library.

I always go there when I've got myself a problem. Been a bit of a reader over the years, you see. The sight of all those books gives me a warm feeling.

Like being surrounded by all your friends, past and present. You know what I mean? History's my subject. Fancy myself as a bit of an expert, too.

I was greeted by my special girl, Iris the librarian. What a smasher she is. Always there with a smile and a joke. Sometimes I wonder whether it's really the books I'm there for.

"Hello, old, sweetie," she whispered. "Aren't you a bit premature?"

"Well, you see, I usually change my books on a Saturday morning. I held out my empty hands and explained that I'd only dropped in for a good think.

"You'll soon have to find a new library," she said. "You've borrowed most of our history section, you know."

"Then I'll start on the fiction." I replied. There was a twinkle in her eye.

"Of course, we do have one famous book you haven't got round to yet."

"Which one's that then?" I enquired. She giggled and pointed behind her. I looked and there was the biggest bundle of pages I'd ever seen.

"That's a book?" I said.

She nodded. "It certainly is. *The Decline and Fall of the Roman Empire*. Go on! I challenge you."

"Couldn't afford the fines on my pension," I said, "and anyway I'll need a wheelbarrow to get it home."

She raised her eyebrows. "You haven't read the D. and F. and you profess to be some kind of expert on history? Huh!"

Well, I know when I'm beaten. "All right," I said. "Wrap it up." She was delighted and laughed as she stamped the inside cover.

"That should keep you occupied for a couple of days. Thirteen centuries of crimes, follies and misfortunes of mankind—or so the catalog says, I'll have it on the counter and you can pick it up as you leave," she said with a giggle.

"If I've got the strength," I said.

I wandered off and found a quiet table—all to myself. Then I sat down and pondered away for a couple of hours.

I watched the people come and go. Pacing up and down—up and

down—until finally they made their choice and left. Leaving me and my problem.

I decided to go home. I was tired and for the first time in my life I felt old. The trouble with me is that I am good in an emergency—but useless when it comes down to scheming schemes.

The book weighed a ton, and all that thinking had worn me out. So by the time I reached the house I fancied a bit of a lie down.

I didn't see Eddie come out of the living room—but as I got to the top of the landing I suddenly heard him shout.

"Dad, can you hear me? I want you to come down this minute! Pat's got something to tell you."

It was when I turned and looked down the stairwell at his smug little face that the giddy spell came on.

Of course, I dropped the book. Well, you see, I had to, otherwise I would have fallen down the stairs. Poor lad, never knew what hit him.

As the policeman said to us later, "At your age it's only to be expected you'll get the odd dizzy turn. You know what I mean?"

Born 1940 in Derby, Sandra Elizabeth Woolley left for London when she was 23 years old. She writes short stories and radio drama and manages an employment service. Miss Woolley was introduced in SSI No. 20 with "Oh for Maisie's Warm Welcome."

"I bought them lunch at the corner deli,
you know, and you should've seen their faces
when I asked for corned beef on rye!"

Saree of the Gods

BY G.S. SHARAT CHANDRA

Complexities of expatriatism.

ONE of the things that Prapulla had insisted was to have a place
waiting for them in New York where other Indian immigrants lived.
She had worried a great deal over this sudden change in her life.
First, there was her fear of flying over Mount Everest, a certain
intrusion over Lord Shiva's territory which he did not approve of for
any believing Hindu. Then the abrupt severance of a generation of
relationships and life in a joint family. She had spent many a restless
night. In daylight, she'd dismiss her nightmares as mere confusions
of a troubled mind and set herself to conquer her problems as she
faced them, like the educated and practical woman that she was. If
anything happened to the transgressing jet, she would clutch her
husband and child to her breasts and plummet with at least a partial
sense of wholeness, to whatever ocean the wrath of the god would
cast her. She would go down like those brave, legendary sea cap-
tains in the history books and movies. But moving over to the West,

where you lived half the year like a monk in a cave because of the weather, was something she was unable to visualize. Besides, how was she going to manage her household without the maid-servant and her stalwart mother-in-law? To be left alone in a strange apartment all day while Shekar went to work was a recurring fear. She had heard that in New York City, even married women wore mini-skirts or leather slacks and thought nothing of being drunk or footloose, not to mention their sexual escapades in summer in parks or parked automobiles. But cousin Manjula who had returned from the States was most reassuring:

"All that is nonsense! Women there are just like women here! Only they have habits and customs quite different from ours. There are hundreds of Indian families in New York. Once you've acclimatized yourself to the country, you'll find it hard to sit and brood. You may run into families from Bangalore in the same apartment house, who knows!"

Prapulla liked the apartment house as soon as she saw some sareed women in the lobby. It was Shekar who looked distraught at the Indian faces. In the time it took for them to arrive from the airport to the apartment, he had seen many of his brown brethren on the city streets, looking strange and out of place. Now he dreaded being surrounded by his kind, ending up like them building little Indias in the obscure corners of New York. He wasn't certain what Prapulla thought about it. She was always quiet on such subjects. Back in India, she was a recluse when it came to socializing and on the few occasions they had entertained foreigners at the firm, she would seek the nearest sofa as a refuge and drop her seven yards of brocade at anchor. She left the impression of being a proper Hindu wife, shy, courteous and traditional.

En route to New York on the jumbo, Shekar had discreetly opened up the conversation about what she'd wear once they were in America. At the mention of skirts she had flared up so defiantly he had to leave the seat. For Prapulla, it was not convenience but convention that made the difference. She had always prized her sarees, especially the occasions she wore her wedding saree with its blue handspun silk and its silver border of gods. There were times she had walked into a crowded room where others were dressed differently and had relished the sudden flush of embarrassment on their faces at her exquisite choice of wear.

The first day of their new life went quite smoothly. When Shekar returned from the office, she was relieved to hear that all had gone well and he had made friends with two of his American colleagues. Shekar described them. Don Dellow was in the firm for fifteen years and was extremely pleasant and helpful. Jim Dorsen and his wife Shirley had always wanted to visit India and shared great interest in the country and its culture.

"I bought them lunch at the corner deli, you know, and you should've seen their faces when I asked for corned beef on rye!" Shekar chuckled. It was during that weekend that Shekar suggested they ought to invite the Dellows and the Dorsens for dinner so she could meet and get to know the wives. Prapulla shrugged her shoulders. It was so soon. She was still unaccustomed to walking into the sterilized supermarkets where you shopped like a robot with a push-cart, led on to the products by where they lay waiting like cheese in a trap, rather than having them beseech you like the vendors and merchants in the bazaars and markets in her country. Besides, everything had a fixed price tag. The frozen vegetables, the canned fruits and spices, the chicken chopped into shapes that were not its own but of the plastic, all bothered her. But Shekar had not complained about her cooking yet. He was so busy gabbing and gulping, she wasn't even sure he knew what was on the plate. Then Shekar walked in from the office Thursday and announced he had invited his friends for dinner on Saturday.

"They both accepted with great delight. It's rather important I develop a strong bond with them."

Prapulla pulled out a pad and started making the shopping list. Shekar was about to ask her what she'd wear but changed his mind.

The Doresens arrived first. Shirley Dorsen introduced herself and immediately took a liking to Prapulla. The Dellows, caught in traffic, came late. Judy Dellow was a lean Spanish woman in her late twenties. She wore a velvet dress with lace cuffs and asked for bourbon. The living room filled with the aroma of spices. In the background, Subbalakshmi recited on the stereo.

"What sort of music is this?" Jim asked, looking somewhat sullen. He had just finished his drink. Shirley was on her fourth.

"Karnatak music," explained Prapulla. "Subbalakshmi is the soprano of South Indian music. She sings mostly devotional songs and lyrics."

"Sounds rather strange and off key to me," said Jim nodding his head in dismay. He sang for the church choir on Sundays.

Shekar announced dinner. He had set the wine glasses next to the handloomed napkins like he had seen in *Good Housekeeping*. As soon as everyone was seated, he abruptly got up. "Gee! I forgot to pour the wine!" he despaired. When he returned, he held an opaque bottle with a long German name.

"What kind of wine is it?" asked Jim.

"The best German riesling there is!" replied Shekar with authority.

"My, you do know your liquor!" said Shirley, impressed.

"Like a book!" quipped Prapulla.

"It's a misconception," Shekar continued hastily, "that French wines are the best. Germans actually mastered the art of wine making long before the French. Besides, you can't beat a German riesling to go with Indian food."

"Excellent!" said Jim. Shekar filled the glasses apologizing again for not having filled them beforehand. "You see, good wine has to be chilled right," he added avoiding Prapulla's unflinching stare. They began to eat. Shirley attacked everything, mumbling superlatives between mouthfuls. Shekar kept a benevolent eye on the plates and filled them as soon as they were empty. Prapulla sat beaming an appropriate smile. When everyone had their fill, Prapulla got up for dessert.

"Is it going to be one of the exotic Indian sweets?" Shirley asked.

"Of course," butted Shekar.

Prapulla returned from the kitchen with Pepperidge Farm turnovers. "Sorry, I had an accident with the *jamoons*," she said meekly.

"Don't worry dear. Turnovers do perfectly well," said Shirley, giving her an understanding look.

Shekar had placed a box of cigars on the coffee table. As they all sat, he offered it to his guests who waved it away in preference to their own crumpled packages of Salem. Don and Jim talked about a contract the firm had lost. A junior engineer from Bombay who used to work for the firm had bungled it. They asked Shekar if he knew the man. Shekar had already stiffened in the chair but he pressed for details. But they veered the conversation away from the topic to compliment him on his choice of brandy.

Prapulla entered with a tray of coffee mixed with cream and sugar, just like back home. Subbalakshmi coughed, cleared her throat and strummed the veena in prayer.

Judy raved about Prapulla's saree. Prapulla, momentarily saved from embarrassment over the coffee, began to explain the ritual importance of the wedding saree. She pulled the upper part from her shoulder and spread it on the table. The silver border with the embroidered legend of the creation of the universe, the different avatars of Lord Shiva and the demons he killed while on earthly mission gleamed under the light. Her favorite one depicted Shiva drinking the poison emitted by the sea serpent with which the universe was churned from the ocean. The Craftsman had even put a knot of gold at Shiva's neck to indicate the poison the god had held in his throat. A sheer triumph of skill.

"With the exception of Shiva as the begging ascetic, the saree-maker has woven all the other avatars. This blank space on the border perhaps is the space left to challenge our imagination!" mused Prapulla. Shirley, with a snifterful of brandy leaned from her chair for a closer look. The brandy tipped. "Oh no!" screamed everyone. Judy ran into the kitchen for a towel but the alcohol hissed like a magical serpent over the saree spreading its poisonous hood. The silver corroded fast and the avatars, disfigured or mutilated, almost merged. Prapulla sat dazed, just staring at her saree. The silence was unbearable. Jim puffed on his pipe like a condemned man. Judy, after trying valiantly to wipe the brandy, bent her head over her hand. Shirley looked red, like she was either going to scream or giggle. Shekar came to the rescue:

"Don't worry. I know a way I can lift the smudges. It's nothing!"

No one believed him. Prapulla abruptly got up and excused

herself.

"I guess we should better be leaving," said Don looking at his watch. "I've to drive the babysitter home and she lives three traffic jams away!"

Shekar hurried to the closet for their coats. "I hope you enjoyed the dinner!" he said meekly, piling up the coats over his shoulder. Prapulla appeared at the door in a different saree. She seemed to have recollected herself and felt bad about everyone leaving so soon. "You know, my husband is right. I've already dipped the saree border in the lotion. It'll be as good as new by morning," she said. They shook hands and Shirley hugged Prapulla and rocked her. "I'll call you dear, let me know how to comes off!" she whispered drunkenly and backed into her coat like an animal perfectly trained.

Prapulla stood at the door with one hand on her stomach, and as the guests disappeared down the elevator, she banged the door shut and ran into the bedroom. She remembered the day she had shopped for the saree. It was a week before her wedding. The entire family had gone to the silk bazaar and spent the day looking for the perfect one. They had at last found it in the only hand-spun saree shop in the market. The merchant had explained that the weaver who had knitted the god into its border had died soon after, taking his craft with him. This was his last saree, his parting gift to some lucky bride. "You modern young people may not believe in old wives tales, but I know that he was a devotee of Shiva. People say the Lord used to appear for him!" the merchant had said.

She sobbed into her shoulders. Where was she going to find a replacement? How was she ever going to explain the tragedy to her family? A wedding saree, selected by the bride became her second self, the sail of her destiny, the roof that protected her and her offsprings from evil. She rushed to Ratri's room to make sure that no mythical serpent or scorpion had already appeared over her daughter's head.

She could hear Shekar washing the dishes in the kitchen and turning the sinkerator that gurgled like a demon with its gulletful of leftovers. She found the impulse to make sure that Shekar had not fallen into it. It was not really Shirley's fault. It was the brandy that her "Americanized" husband kept pouring into her glass. He was so imitative and flippant, lavishing food and liquor that they could scarcely afford on people that were yet to be called friends. He had drunk more than he should have as if to prove that he held his liquor well enough to win points for promotion! Who really discovered brandy? Shekar had brackishly turned the picture of Napoleon on the bottle toward his guests, but surely it must have been a demon who despised her or was sent to convey the god's displeasure at her mixed company, her expatriatism.

She grew tired of her mind's hauntings. There was no way to change the events or turn back now. When Ratri grew up, she would cut the saree and make a dress for her. She'd write to her mother-in-law and send money for a special puja at the temple.

In her dream, it was her funeral. Four priests carried her on bamboo. The family walked behind. Shekar, dressed in traditional dhoti walked ahead with the clay vessel of hot coals with which he'd kindle the first spark of fire. The procession moved briskly to the crematory grounds. A pyre was built and her corpse decked with her favorite flowers was laid on top. Someone tied the border of the saree firmly to a log. The bereaved went around chanting the necessary hymns and the priests sprinkled holy water over her. Suddenly she was ablaze. She felt nothing but an intense heat around her. The flames did not seem to touch her. She pinched herself. She was not on the pyre but was standing with her family. It was her wedding saree wrapped around a giant bottle of brandy that was burning! Inside the bottle a demon danced, spitting fire. The avatars slowly uncurled from the silver border like an inflated raft and ascended the smoke. They were all in miniature, fragile in their postures and luminous. The brandy in the bottle foamed and swirled like an ocean. The demon raved in its ring of fire. Prapulla screamed. One of the uncles gently touched her on the arm and said:

"Do not be alarmed. The demon points its tongue upwards. The gods have flown to their proper heaven."

When she woke herself from the nightmare, Shekar was soundly snoring on the bedside. The sky outside hung in a spent, listless grayness. She could see a haze of light back of a skyscraper. Dawn would soon brim the horizon of her new world with neither birds nor the song of priests in the air. She sat in the dark of the living room

49

with the saree on her lap, caressing its border absentmindedly. A brittled piece broke and fell.

Born in 1935 in Mysore, India, G.S. Sharat Chandra was educated as a lawyer and taught law until 1967 when he made the decision to abandon law for literature. His short stories and poetry are published around the world. He has taught English literature and creative writing at universities in several countries. At last contact, he was seeking to again be associated with a university as he misses the liveliness and stimulation of students.

"I thought you wouldn't want me to . . . to look.
I mean . . . you know, your wounds . . ."

The Return

BY SHAMMAI GOLAN

Faces of courage.

THE bouquets came with noisy bustle. There were roses and gladioli
and carnations and wild chrysanthemums. Eitan maneuvered
among them in his wheelchair, his hands white against the wheels.
Many visitors had come to welcome him like a bridgegroom, their
eyes on the bouquets in their hands. He too turned his weary eyes to
the flowers. Good thing they hadn't brought them wreathed and
wrapped in bright cellophane—that kind gets put on fresh graves,
and he, after all, was completely healthy. Through his swollen face
he saw them coming in, in twos and threes, as if wearing tags of
delegations. Here were Alex and Simon Kalmanovitz from the Interior Trade Bank, necktied and framed in starched-collared shirts.
The apartment-house tenants' committee also appeared in full com-
plement as to a tenants' meeting, a cream cake going before them in
the hands of Mrs. Tirosh. His regiment liaison officer with his sec-
retary apologized that the regiment commander hadn't been able to

come, for the regiment had been demobilized quite some time ago, and only the wounded, like Eitan, had remained on active service. Representatives also came from the Rehabilitation Bureau and from the Friday tennis club and from the young people's section of the party branch. When they expressed their sorrow about his being wounded so severely their faces were grave as if it were their fault, they even tried to cheer him with slaps on the shoulder, saying he had recovered now and was home again. He didn't encourage them with a smile of lips or words of politeness. Through his sealed eyelashes he heard their chatter and the sucking as they drank.

"Feel bad?" asked Nilli, and before he answered she declared, "Eitan feels perfectly fine!" She folded his hands on his chest: "Leave those wheels alone, Eitan!" She repeated his name severely, with the stress on the last syllable. Bet that's how she scolds her pupils when they're bad.

They left furtively, pressing hand to hand to wish success and vanished behind the heavy door. Mother and Father, too, wished him a complete recovery and hinted that they didn't want to disturb the young couple on their first day.

The silence was harder than the noise. Then came the sound of dishes in the sink. The doorway, narrower than his wheelchair, blocked his path to the kitchen. The water streamed strongly, pouring over the plastic dishes. He took up his crutches and hobbled into the kitchen. His strange legs dragged along. He wanted to embrace her from behind, as on his night on leave, but he didn't have the strength. He knew that if he let go his crutches he'd collapse on the floor. Again he relived that stolen evening.

He appeared with his weapon and his duty clothes. His chapped lips hurt as he smiled at her laughing eyes. He'd come for a little while, he said, he was on his way from Command Headquarters to the Jordan Valley. She came into his arms, soft, and his hands lacked patience. You're hurting me, she giggled. During long summer nights of ambushes he'd imagined this moment. It's all so sudden, she grasped his hands as if protecting herself. Maybe you'll eat something, she suggested.and we should wake the children so you can say hello to them. She straightened her scattered hair and slipped by him into the kitchen. He stuck to her in the kitchen. Will

you have a shower, she asked. I wasn't prepared at all . . . He filled
his hands with her breasts. The sheets are clean, Eitan . . . His
breathing was heavy, his body broke into her body and he was a
stranger to himself. He frightened himself. Afterwards he apologized.
When they sat down to drink coffee, he apologized. In that blazing
Valley a man loses his humanity, turning into an animal in a herd of
males. The nights are long, Nilli, even in summer, and they're hot.
We speak very little in that heat. The instincts, Nilli, the senses, they
develop the way they do in an animal. A man-animal. The hunger for
a woman, when you're lying in ambush, stuck to the hot earth. Lying
there unmoving. Because if they find you first, as we say and laugh, it
isn't worth it . . . He spoke fervently, trying to find out what she
thought, to break her silence. Once we ran into them, and one of
them managed to get in among us with a hand grenade. He ran
around inside the circle like a trapped animal. The grenade in his
hand. We took care not to hit him at such short range. The grenade,
you understand, that was the danger. Let him fuck himself, not us.
Animals, eh? One gets used to it. You even fall asleep while you're in
ambush. You fall asleep, in the presence of death. And when you
finally get on the half-track, you still stay silent. Only towards noon
does speech come. It bursts out all at once. With the plate of soup
and the flies and the mites and the sweat. What do you know about
it? He gripped her shoulders and tried to turn her face to his. Until we
start playing "If only." If only I were at home. If only the refrigerator
were here. If only the woman. The woman the woman the woman.
All the visions raised in the tent. You can sense the lust steaming
behind the words. Words masturbate, Nilli, have you ever heard of
words masturbating? This deserves thought, Eitan, said Nilli. She
stressed the last syllable, and said no more. He thought he heard her
voice scolding him, like the kids in her class. Soon she'd say: Fold
you arms, Eitan.

For a long while he stood in the kitchen doorway, his head
lowered and his hands tight on the grips until they hurt.

The wide bed was strange to him. Nilli lay beside him. From her
hands came the smell of dish-soap. Beneath his hesitant fingers her
body was like crutches which required re-learning. The smell of that
soap. Couldn't she have used some cologne, some of the cologne

he'd brought her from the army store? Her eyes were fixed on the ceiling. If she'd only put out a hand to his body. If he could only feel her fingers touching him.

"You don't even look at me," he said in desperation.

She gazed at a hidden spot on the ceiling and whispered: "I thought you wouldn't want me to . . . to look. I mean . . . you know, your wounds . . ."

"I know," he bit his lips.

"You don't know a thing!" she flung at him.

"Perhaps," he said very meaningfully and pulled the blanket over his head. Like when he was little, after Mother had gone and he stuffed his ears with the softness of the blanket. So as not to hear the secret sounds from the corners of the room. He turned over and placed his stomach carefully on the mattress. The weariness gathered in his bones. He dreamed that he had to run somewhere on an important mission. His mother had ordered him to get to Ha-Nevi'im Street. He had to hurry, but he couldn't. His crutches were a burden. He awoke in alarm. He passed his hand over his forehead. The hand was moist. He glanced at his wife. Her face was yellow in the light of the nightlamp. Her hair surrounded her face in a black halo.

"The office asked when you'd be back," he heard her voice. She spoke as if she were talking to herself. Perhaps it was her voice that had woken him. "You still had six days to go until your release," she continued without looking at him. "Soon, I told them. Don't keep him to yourself, they said on the phone." He saw her lips open into a smile. Maybe it was she who had commanded him to run. He wanted to show her. "I have no right to keep him to myself, I said to them." Now she looked at him. Her brown eyes were sad. Like in moments of reconciliation after anger. The doctor who'd told him to say nothing—he was smart. He always felt guilty before her. Her sad eyes proclaimed his guilt. He noticed a spark of pity in them. He shut his eyes. Let her think he's sleeping. If she puts her fingers on his eyelids, he'll kiss them with his eyelashes. They're probably as cold as a pillow after Mother's changed the pillowcase.

"You didn't tell me how it happened. Did it hurt? Does it still hurt?" Conjugations of the Hebrew verb to hurt. A teacher is always a teacher, she often boasted. "The children are so naughty. Since you went they became wild. And when you didn't come back . . . they made up a song." (She forgot that she'd already told him their song while he was lying in hospital) "Abba-ba-be-heli (Daddy came in a heli[copter])." She sang it softly, her lips moving slowly. She raised herself on her elbows. "Their eyes scare me, Eitan. Ronni's eyes glint so. Scheming," she spoke quickly. He noticed her breast through the opening of her shirt and again sensed his helplessness. "You know, when Ronni wears the jeans you bought him before you went to reserves service, he looks like a little man. You're lonely, Mother, he says. I'll never leave you all by yourself. If you like, I'll sleep in the big bed instead of Father."

He couldn't bear her words. Let her stop. Let the silence return. He was so weary. He saw her sitting up. Just don't let her come to the stumps of his legs. Every movement of hers in the bed drove him crazy. Any minute now she'd sit on his ankles that weren't there any more, and promise to be nice to him. "I know you're listening, Eitan. And you're not speaking." She placed a hand gently on his shoulder. Mechanical recoil. Let Ronni sleep in his bed, he spoke to her without opening his mouth.

"Nilli," he said softly, "Nilli, I'll be all right."

"I know, Eitan," she kissed him on his forehead. The smell of that soap. He felt a spasm of nausea. With a trembling hand he switched off the nightlamp and turned his back to her.

In the morning he saw Nilli approach with awe and place a cup of coffee beside his bed. From the corner of his eye he caught her glance. She retreated with hasty steps.

"Do I frighten you?" he asked softly.

"What are you talking about?" she came back to him hesitantly.

"You ran off," he didn't leave off.

"Your eyes . . ." she stammered.

"I frightened you!" he shouted. She moved away again. But he didn't leave off. "I didn't ask for coffee in bed," he pursued her with his voice, "I'm not sick!" He felt as if his wounds were opening up again. She came back and reached a hand out to the cup. Then he grasped her upper arm. "Sit here a minute," he asked-commanded. She passed one hand over his scarred thigh. "You know," he spoke to the arm, "after the mine exploded, I was fully conscious. And I thought, well it's happened to me. Then I thought how would I live without legs. At that moment I was even curious. And then I wanted to die. And you?" He asked suddenly. He pursed his lips in anticipation.

"Me?" she stammered, and tried to get up.

"You didn't run into a mine;" he didn't let go her arm. Her fingers were hard, they hurt his thigh. "Only I did it;" he hoped for a word of consolation, but she didn't speak. "I want you to know it the way I know it," he said in a gentle tone.

"Of course, I'll learn," she pulled her hand away and put it beside her thigh.

"How?" he asked, struggling to hide his disappointment.

"The way you tell me," she spoke drily.

"Come," he pulled her waist.

"What're you doing, Eitan, it's already morning. My work . . ."

"Come," he didn't let up.

"Right away," she said. "I'll just go and turn off the stove."

When the doorbell rang she came back. "I'll be right back," she said and vanished. He heard the door opening, and dulled voices.

"Why are you whispering there?" he called out. His voice echoed strangely in the house.

Nilli came running back. "It's the milkman, Eitan, you don't want us not to have milk in the house, do you?" She spoke like a teacher.

He sat erect, vainly trying to quiet his anger.

"The doctor said you mustn't . . ." she began.

"I know myself what I may and what I mustn't," he stated.

She smiled to him. "Of course, Eitan. Since when does my Eitan follow doctor's orders." She sat down on the edge of the bed and raised his chin. "Laws were created by the weak for the weak, remember?"

"But we spit on them and on their laws," he laughed aloud.

"That's exactly what you said," she spoke more excitedly now, "their laws. And you spoke that whole bombastic sentence just to kiss me in that café, in the face of all the eyes in the world. A department manager of the Interior Trade Bank and a teacher at a government school," she laughed, "and parents to two children.

How exemplary," again she smoothed his chin.

"You promised to come right back!" he suddenly changed his tone. He was an interrogator. He demanded a reply.

"But I'm here, Eitan," she moved on the bed as if afraid to hurt him. "This evening we'll go out, to the movies," she added, as if sharing a secret.

"To the movies!" he yelled, rejecting.

"Why not?"

"So everyone can look at us and pity us . . ."

"Are you scared?" she teased him.

Again he grasped her arm. All his anger was now concentrated between his fingers.

"You're not going to prove anything like *that*," she said, and pulled her arm away.

He let go and leaned back against the wall. "What'll I do, what'll I do, what'll I *do*," he repeated, demanding an answer.

"Start everything over," she said. It sounded like a slogan.

"Like in the old days," he scoffed.

"Like in the old days," she affirmed, nodding her head.

"To court you," he said roughly.

"Court me," she said.

"Without legs," he pointed to his stumps, and laughed bitterly.

"To court me you don't need legs." Her face was severe.

"You don't pity me," he let out, surprisingly.

"I can pity you a week or two," she spoke as if thinking aloud. "After that I'll hate you."

"Start with pity. After that we'll see," he tried to chuckle. He passed his hand through her hair and pulled her to him and kissed her on her eyelids and lips.

"Eitan," she whispered, hard.

"You're my wife . . ."

"So what? my husband." Wicked barbs flashed for a moment in her eyes, and flickered out.

"Nilli," he said, "Nilli . . ." trying to placate her, "you know how much I wanted to come home!" He stopped and looked at her lowered head. "The doctors said that it was this powerful desire, that's what they said, this powerful desire, that healed me. You know it, this desire," he chuckled. "For bachelors, they said, it's harder, because they don't have a home and a wife who cares for them and children to amuse them. A mother, they said, is only a mother, she's not a woman like a man needs . . ."

"They were right," she cut him off. "The house is ready, you see?" She motioned with her arm. "I even sent the children to my parents . . ."

"I know, Nilli, I know," he stopped talking and put his body deep under the blanket. He pulled it up to his neck, and it was still long. "But," he suddenly said bitterly, "you don't have to prove anything to a mother. And Mother'll keep on saying how good I was at school and how the headmaster said at the ceremony that I was strong in math, I solved problems in algebra and when I was a baby crawling on fours I no longer wet my bed and Mother . . ."

"Mother . . ." she cut him off contemptuously.

When he lay in hospital he planned his return home. And then, in the convalescent ward, he planned. As soon as they were alone he'd prove himself to her. It was important to him, to prove. He'd come on his crutches, and prove. The doctors had promised him that he was fine. They wouldn't have sent him otherwise. They put him in a wheelchair and placed his crutches beside him. The nurse had giggled. Her arms, supporting him under the armpits, were naked. And her shoulder was soft. He was in awe of her naked flesh. When she bent her head over him he always marveled at the golden plume of hair at the ends of her black curls. Come on, Eitan, she encouraged him as he climbed into the ambulance on his way home, as if he were about to shoot a goal.

Nilli passed her hand through his hair and said gently, "Your certificate of release from the hospital says that you're a hundred per cent fit."

"That's right," he hastened to confirm her words, "I'm a hundred per cent fit." By the smile quavering at the corners of her lips he knew her thoughts. Her eyes trembled. She passed her hand under her nose. Like Talli when she cries. He wanted to feel her cheek on his chest. To hear her whisper softly, murmuring it didn't matter what. Like her soft steps when he first noticed her as she came into his hospital room. Possibly she'd come lots of times, and he hadn't known. Through the bandages, which left narrow spaces for his eyes, he saw her come in. Holding a bunch of flowers like at a funeral. First she arranged the flowers in a vase, then spread the rest around his head so he could smell them whenever he liked. Their friends hadn't wanted to trouble him, so they'd sent the flowers with her, she'd said. Then she'd sat down at his feet, and he'd felt himself very small without feet. A baby in diapers and necktie. From the moment she came he hadn't stopped repeating that stupid sentence to himself: She's mine she's mine she's mine. The words were fixed in his heart, like a prayer. The doctor ordered him to keep quiet, and he was happy keeping quiet. The doctor and his prohibitions. He could have ordered him not to walk. But when he signed the release certificate, he ordered him to walk and talk and have a good time. The plump doctor with the thick lips and the Anglo-Saxon accent: Okay fellow you're fine, you're one hundred per cent. Nilli spoke, telling about the helicopter. He was glad that his ears remained outside the bandages, though they too had been hurt in the explosion. They protruded and were yellow, like horns. How are my ears, he'd wanted to shout out. The helicopter had flown direct to Hadassah, Nilli had said. It was hard to live or imagine it. From the Jordan Valley a direct flight. The red lights in its belly. Like wounds. Three soldiers wounded, the Army spokesman had announced. I knew you were among them. They didn't say slight or medium or heavy wounds. I knew it was you.

She was his Nilli, Nilli whom he wanted even as he writhed in pain. Everytime the helicopter flew above the house, she told him, she would run out onto the balcony. Even in her sleep she would see the blades of the propellors. Striking and landing on the roof of our house. She opened her purse with practiced fingers and pulled out a tiny mirror. I knew that a helicopter arriving at night could only be bringing wounded. She stopped and looked at Eitan, and without looking at the mirror put it back in the purse. She moved on the bed, and he felt a sharp pain in his feet. In the place where his feet had been. You're hallucinating, he calmed himself. Her eyes wandered across the white screen the nurse had put up to give them privacy, as if insisting on their intimacy. As was right for a husband and wife after a long separation. Or perhaps she had feared Nahshon's blind eyes.

When the helicopter passes over the house, the children sing heli-heli-heli-copter. I scold them and tell them it's got a Hebrew name. It's got a belly like a frog, they sing. It's silly, thinking of an inanimate thing like that. They don't distinguish between inanimate and animate things. When it passes over us, I wait for the phone to ring. I'm always ready. The children know. That's why they call out: Mother, a helicopter. Quiet, children, I say, and repeat the Hebrew name. But helicopter's nicer, they plead, it's so heli-heli-heli. They've made up a dance. And they sing it to a nursery tune heli-heli-heli . . .

"The nurse in the hospital," he suddenly said, "she did a dance in front of Nahshon's bed. She had blond hair on the nape of her neck. And Nahshon was blind, blind," he repeated, "and she danced until Nahshon started clapping his hands to the rhythm of her feet." He stopped for a moment and continued in a low voice, his eyes seeking in vain for his wife's glance, "to the same rhythm. He-li . . ."

"They don't announce any details about the wounded," said Nilli, ignoring what he'd said. "Not their age, not their names. All they announce is that a vehicle hit a mine somewhere south of . . . or east of . . . or west of . . . As if the direction was what mattered. But now the nightmare's over." She made her voice sound gay. "See?" she added, flouncing her earrings, "I've made myself pretty." The veins in her neck were like a pair of cords.

When she came to the hospital she'd been wearing the earrings. Why earrings, Mother, she'd imitated Talli's voice. I've put perfume on my body for you. She had moved her body closer to his bandaged face so he could smell it and he had turned his head away. You like perfume, she'd said angrily, and wiped her eyes with a handkerchief. If you smile, Eitan, I'll know that you still love me. It doesn't matter. You don't have to. What matters is that I'm sitting beside you. Talli said, I want to too. You know the children, they want everything.

"The children!" he suddenly cried joyfully.

"They'll come tomorrow. I thought you might want to rest a day or two." She spoke in an offended tone.

"The children!" he repeated stubbornly.

"Today?"

"Now," he spoke fervently, "right away, you have to go at once, and bring them."

He had been sure that they would change everything.

He was sitting in an armchair when the children came. It seemed that his lack was not apparent through his polished shoes. Nevertheless they were in fear of approaching him. Ronni dared and kissed him on his shaven cheek and wiped his lips and asked if Daddy had brought sweets from the army store. As if he was reciting a sentence he had learned by heart. Then he made the crutches into ladders and started ascending and descending, calling out: I'm taller. Talli didn't even kiss him. She sat in his wheelchair and looked at him through the fair hair flowing over her forehead. He beckoned to her to come to him. But she withdrew in between the sides of the wheelchair and shook her head stubbornly from left to right. He explained to her how to release the handbrake and how to move the wheels. Nilli encouraged her: "Come on, Talli, ride to Daddy. Come on, Talli, remember?" She started singing: "Daddy came in a heli . . ." and gently pushed the wheelchair. Talli fell. Her nose started bleeding, and his legs were too short to help her. Nilli washed Talli's face and didn't urge her any more.

During the days that followed he enveloped himself in silence, as if still bound by the doctor's order. In the morning, still lying on the folding guest-bed (he had insisted on their sleeping apart until the pain went away) he would hear Nilli preparing the children for school and kindergarten. Finally they went out, Ronni and Talli on either side of her like a pair of bodyguards, Ronni's arm in his mother's in the manner of his father. Then the stillness returned, and there was no point in getting up any more. He only doddered to their large bed, still warm from his wife's body, breathed in deeply and dived under the blanket. Like Ronni and Talli when he was still in the army. It was they who had consecrated the bed. Before he'd left for Reserves Service they'd ordered this new bed from the carpenter. Until the mattresses arrived it had stood empty. Like an open plank cupboard, Nilli had tried to make him laugh while he was in hospital. But then she rolled her upper lip over her lower one and said: the bed stood there like a swimming pool. And Ronni and Talli broke it in by swimming breaststroke and backstroke and sidestroke in it because you Eitan are a bad boy and you didn't take them to the pool. She spoke in a pampered voice. Had she kept that tone up, the bed might have become a pool for him too. But here it was too stifling, and he crawled out and placed his stumps into their stocks and set out on a journey through the apartment. His movements were still clumsy, and he took care not to damage the statuettes. The glass and porcelain vases also tried to deter him. He stopped only in the children's room, and sat down to rest on the striped rug. Here he had used to slide Ronni from his knees, arched like a bridge, down to the soles of his bare feet. Yo-ho, Ronni's yelling of the Indian motto still echoed in the air. Eitan stretched out on his back. With the aid of his hands he gathered and raised his knees, and they gazed back at him accusingly. Until he pounded his fists into them in furious silence.

At lunch time too he was silent. During the first days he tried to entertain his children. From the bread he made birds' heads and human feet. Nilli said it's wrong to spoil bread, and he obeyed her. Then they lay down to rest. A new custom Nilli had introduced, afternoon naps, siesta, she said. She'd learned it from the deputy headmaster, who had recently returned from a tour of duty for the Jewish Agency in some South American country. Eitan should understand, she's a working person, pupils' books to mark, lessons to prepare, and Ronni and Talli don't make it any easier. They've become wild. Savages. The deputy headmaster calls Ronni to his office from time to time, and scolds him in the presence of his mother the teacher. What's needed in this house is the firm hand of a man. So, children, off to bed.

And again he remains alone in the armchair, scanning the afternoon paper. The alarm clock ticks its time and leads to the hour when his wife will wake, and he will again remain alone. His eyes flit over the pages of the newspaper, until they find what they're looking for. At first he tries to interpret, through the letters inside the black frames, who has died a hero's death and who has simply fallen in the course of duty. The distinction is clear. The wounded are not mentioned by name. At least his own name should have appeared. Like, say, The community of workers of the Interior Trade Bank extend their condolences to Nilli and her children on the untimely loss of the feet of their dear and beloved Eitan Keren (Krasnilsky), or, deeply grieve over the wounding of our friend Sergeant Eitan Keren may the Lord avenge his blood whose feet were taken in the prime of his life, and extend condolences to the family. (signed) His friends in the tennis club; or, to Nilli Keren and family: shocked at the wounding of your husband Eitan, from your colleagues Jorge-Yosef (acting headmaster) and staff.

The fly striking the glass of the window pane cuts short his thoughts, dulls his senses, and he sinks into a troubled sleep. Like in the half-track, coming back from ambush at night, the lights of the camp winking in the distance. The noise that he hears is the alarm clock waking Nilli. He can hear her getting up. Her uncombed head appears for a moment in the doorway and vanishes. Then water streaming and the rubbing of the toothbrush. As if it were morning now, and she getting herself ready for her day's work. Very noisily he folds the newspaper. So she can hear the rustling of the pages, and come. But she doesn't come. She's hurrying to dress the children. So they can have time to play outside and come back to watch television at six. Robin Hood starts at six sharp. We have to be strong, she says. To keep going, as if nothing's happened. Father said that's how we ought to be. Nilli's still wrapped up in her father. The father has a jewelry shop, and she's his only daughter. Maybe she's still angry at Eitan for not agreeing to go to the synagogue with her father that Saturday morning. Since the last war the father's been attending synagogue. Our days have been renewed as of old. And you young people don't grasp the essence of these profound times. It was early on a Saturday morning, and the next day he was to leave for Reserves Service. He knew her thoughts and he said, Three wars, Nilli, and no one scratch, and not one synagogue. Let them go, your old man and his profound times; he laughed, and stripped off his pajamas. He stretched himself before her as if wanting to prove the masculinity of his limbs. The children, Nilli said in alarm, they might suddenly come in. He pulled her to him and laughed in her ear: Mustn't be ashamed of the naked truth. She tried to slip out of his embrace; Father's waiting. With his naked feet he held down her ankles. Then he saw her lips twist in contempt, you can't get everything with feet. Since when did Eitan obey orders? He sat up, when she'd slipped out from under him, surveying his body, making the muscles of his chest and stomach dance, as if tempting her. For your sake, Eitan, she pleaded. Don't worry about me, Nilli, Eitan knows what's good for him. He sat there, looking again at the muscles of his arms. Yesterday I won the tennis club championship, and next year I'll get to be branch manager. When he saw her disappointment, he ran his hand down her back. When I get to your father's age, I'll go to synagogue too, he solemnly promised. You're unbearable, she said, responding to his traveling fingers. They both laughed. Whenever she feels herself vanquished, she says: You're unbearable.

Now for sure she's cutting a cucumber into four horizontal strips and chopping them on the board like the body of a carp. Taking care of his diet. Because he sits all day his body tends to fat, she explained to him, so he mustn't eat starches. Salads have to be his main nourishment. Lots of salads. Or he has to stop sitting and reading. You're hooked on newspapers like on drugs. What's in there that you haven't read yesterday. They just stuff your mind. Fables and commentaries. He ought to read something serious. Some periodical, or journal. If he likes she'll bring one from the staff room. There's a shelf full there. The deputy headmaster subscribed to them all. Even supplements. He should read a serious book. One that deals with the real man.

"Nilli," he suddenly called, "I've found a serious book!" He'd found it this morning during his sail through the rooms. On the first leaf it said: To the outstanding trainee Eitan Keren, from the commander. of the snipers' course.

"A book, Nilli!" He read the inscription again and felt the veins bulging in his neck. His stomach hurt when he laughed. But he didn't give up. "Want to hear what it says inside?" Now he no longer waited for an answer. He opened the book and started reading: "Until relatively recently (the beginning of the 60s) it was customary to define a fatal splinter (one capable of killing a man) as one which at the moment of impact has an energy of some 8kg./meter. It now appears that this criterion is unrealistic, since there are additional factors which are decisive with regard to the capacity of a splinter (or a bullet) to kill or maim. Of two bullets or splinters with the same potential energy but of different shape—one flat and the other shaped like a thin arrow— the thin arrow will penetrate the body and cause serious internal damage or even death much more easily than the flat splinter. As an analogy, imagine what would happen if we took two weights, each of

1 kg., one of them pointed and sharp like a stake and the other shaped like a broad plate, and carried them to a height of 8 meters and dropped them on two people standing below. It is clear that the unfortunate person on whom the narrow weight falls has a much greater chance of being split into two, while the other has a much greater chance of coming out unhurt or with no more than superficial bruises or fractures."

When he raised his eyes, he saw Nilli leaning on the doorjamb, one hand holding the plate of salad, the other in the pocket of her apron. "Have you finished?" she asked, not moving. Her voice was hard.

"You wanted me to read a serious book," he looked at her with a mocking expression.

"I only asked if you've finished," her teeth remained clenched, and her cheeks were taut and pale. She looked beautiful with that pallor.

"Not yet." He lowered his head to the book, moistened his finger and turned the page. "A more precise criterion, accepted today, states that the capacity of a splinter or bullet to kill depends on the quantity of energy per unit of surface which the splinter forces into the body. The concensus today is that a splinter which strikes a body, 'producing' at impact an energy of 17 kg./meter over a surface of 1 sq. cm, is fatal. But this statement too is not complete. And it is also possible that a splinter which on this definition is unable to kill may cause death by a hit in essential organs, like the eyes, the heart, and so on. The place where the splinter or bullet hits the body is thus an additional factor which determines whether the hit is fatal or only wound-producing." Without changing the tone of his voice, he added, "What do you think, Nilli, is my wound fatal or only wound-producing? For it says here in the book . . ."

The three of them were looking at him. He could *hear* their gazes. They were sitting still in their chairs, the plates before them, their eyes on him. Talli had a thumb in her mouth, a forefinger plucking her eyebrow. Ronni was swinging his feet impatiently, and Nilli just looked at him.

"The television," he closed the book with a bang. "I completely forgot." He rolled his chair to the table. Since his return from hospital they'd been eating in the large room, so that his wheelchair too could come to the table. He pinched at the bread and said: "The hero who will soon appear on the screen."

"Robin Hood," Ronni finally burst out. "Every arrow he shoots is a bullseye, Dad."

"A hit," said Eitan.

"A hit for sure, Dad."

"You want to hear about a hit, son?" He bent forward and opened the book again.

"I really do, Dad." His son folded his right leg under his left, ready to listen.

Eitan sensed his wife's resentful gaze on the nape of his neck, but he started reading. "A hit on the body produces two principal kinds of results, one of which has a transitory effect on the body, while the other's effect is permanent. When the body is hit, a 'cone of pressure' is created which strongly compresses the tissues and limbs in the vicinity of the point of entry. The pressure area returns to its normal state after the bullet has passed through it if it did not contain any essential organs (like nerves, major blood vessels and so on). But if any essential organs were present in the area of influence of this 'pressure cone,' permanent damage occurs. Another result of a hit which can be clearly distinguished is the path traced by the bullet on its passage through the body; along this path organs and tissues are torn, and permanent damage is caused which does not disappear with the passing of the bullet or splinter except perhaps a long time later (when the wounded man recovers), and often it remains forever." He closed the book quietly. He knew that he remained alone beside the table. Nilli was already busy cleaning the house for tomorrow. She cleaned the house in the evenings. Eitan had to sit by the window until she finished. The dust disturbed his breathing. Why doesn't he go out a bit. Breathe some fresh air. No one would notice him go. The children, at this hour, were busy following the exploits of their hero. The arrow their hero shot never missed its mark because the right was on his side.

Later in the evening Nilli went out. She wouldn't be home late, she promised. The teachers' meetings had been planned in advance. All properly scheduled. The deputy headmaster likes order. A starting time and a finishing time. The children wouldn't bother him, for she's already put them to bed. And they know they mustn't bother their father. Even if Talli wets her bed (suddenly she's started wetting again) she'll fall asleep after crying a little. So he has no responsibilities. Except that he can't fall asleep at nights. The nights are long and drag on like the hours of ambush in the Valley, like the mined dirt-tracks.

He doddered to the bathroom. He still had to wash himself before Nilli left for the meeting. The wounds on his chest and stomach troubled him in the absence of Nilli's gentle fingers. He took off his clothes and waited. The tiled walls were white, like the hospital walls. His eyes wandered around until they came to his private parts. The water in the bath was shallow, and his public hairs floated like the arms of a jellyfish. Jellyfish, he named himself again as he sat in the tepid and oily soapy water. Jellyfish, he blurted again, and peered at the folds of his scarred stomach. The splinters were fatal or only wound-producing. You're healthy, Eitan, healthy like an oily green jellyfish, which cleaves to its disgusting life. You have to decide, Eitan, you have to decide what you are.

"You could have told me you were in the bath," said Nilli. He sensed her fury through her fingers rubbing his body with the green sponge. Fingers of soap. Green. Sticky. Arms of a jellyfish. He bent forward, his hands on his thighs. A better position for breathing. You can live with this. All you have to do is bend deeper and keep on breathing and absorbing your wife's fingers.

He opened the faucet and pointed the cold water at his face.

"How dumb can you be, Eitan," yelled Nilli and jumped aside. She came around to face him and stood there bewildered, shaking the water from her apron. She always wore the plastic apron when she came to help him wash. It's practical, she explained. Now she wiped her face with the edge of the apron and found herself smearing the water over the layer of make-up. How will she go to the meeting, he thought. "You could've at least warned me!" she added.

"A jellyfish doesn't talk." He closed the faucet and chuckled.

"Don't be a bad boy, Eitan." She still stood at a distance, hesitating, and he looked at her tanned, naked, legs.

"The wheelchair," he blurted, as if suddenly remembering. "Talli'll fall again."

She came up to him and started passing the hairy towel across his shoulders. "She won't fall again," she said confidently.

"One could turn the wheelchair into a jellyfish," he said. The towel hovered in the air for an instant.

"Of course one could, Eitan." Again he heard the bewilderment in her voice, the dread.

"A green one," he added.

"A green one," she repeated and gripped his arm, trying to help him climb out.

He pushed her aside with his elbow. "I'll manage by myself."

"Eitan!" she called out severely.

He raised himself on his hands and thrust the lower part of his body out of the tub. He felt a pleasure at the way the muscles of his neck bulged while his body was in mid-air. If he wanted, he could grasp her thin neck and feel the pulsing of her veins as they slowed and dimmed.

He heard the door slam and her voice from behind it: "If you need me . . ."

He burst through the door. Leaping on all fours, encircling the fleeing ankles of his wife, his right hand supporting her back lest she fall. Through his fingers he sensed her astonishment. Her body froze for a moment and then began a silent struggle. The more she twisted in his arms the greater was his desire. His right hand slid down along her spine and the desire flowed from his fingertips to his loins.

"I'm late for my meeting, Eitan," she said.

"The children'll hear," she pleaded.

"Not here," she said, bending to him, and he kissed her on the lips.

"The light's too strong, Eitan." Suddenly she helped his feverish hands to undo her clothes.

"You're heavy," she ran her hand along his body to the ends of his stumps.

"My green jellyfish," she whispered in his ear.

Afterwards he lay beside her weary, the floor under his back, a triumphant smile on his lips. His eyes did not cease traveling over her naked body.

"Cover me," she requested.

"Why?" he teased.

"I must be very ugly in this light."

"Mustn't be ashamed of the naked truth," he laughed. "Remember?"

"You know yourself," she passed her hand over his face, "that two births don't add beauty to a woman's body."

"I know." He sat, not shifting his gaze.

"The scar on my stomach . . . that's from Talli." She spoke in a faint voice. "Remember? She was big. And on her side too." She took his hand and placed it on her stomach as if trying to cover it.

"Everyone has a scar of his own," he said, in a joking voice.

They burst out laughing. Quietly. Lest the children hear them.

The prominent Israeli writer Shammai Golan was born in Poland in 1933. He experienced Nazi occupation and exile in Cyprus before entering Israel in 1947. He was educated in a kibbutz and at Hebrew University. Since 1971 Mr. Golan has been serving as Director General of the Writers' House in Jerusalem. Mr. Golan was Chairman of the P.E.N. World-Wide Conference held in Jerusalem in 1974. His literary awards include the coveted Agnon Prize for Literature, Asher Barash Prize, ACUM Prize, Ramat-Gan Prize and the Walenrod Award of the Hebrew Writers' Association. Richard Flantz, editor of Modern Hebrew Literature, *translated the story.*

"Whenever I was with my brother
and listened to him, I was certain that father
was at fault."

Caught in the Middle

BY SHAHNON AHMAD

Fences of traditions.

ONCE again a misunderstanding erupted between my father and my older brother. This time both of them were unyielding. Neither was willing to put up the white flag. Father had been this way most of his life; mother often told me how stubborn he had been when he was younger. Father was hardheaded, unwilling to give in even when he knew he was in the wrong. But this time the situation was even worse: his own son had become his enemy. Father would rather die than give in; and my brother was nearly as stubborn and hardheaded as my father. The old folks have a saying: "The shadow of a tree follows the shape of the tree." Nothing is more difficult than trying to reconcile two stubborn men. It's worse even than trying to bring peace between two powerful nations at war. To add to it all, the men involved were my own father and brother.

I was caught right in the middle, unable to bend to the left or to the right. I was in a dilemma; I didn't know what to do. Every time I returned home to our village, my father would grumble and say mean and terrible things about my brother: "Don't ever do like your brother. It was not enough for him to marry a European woman; he had to marry a damned sterile one at that! And now he's adopted a Chinese boy. I wonder what he looks like. Your brother must feel pretty proud to have a European wife, but who made it possible for him to get where he is today? I did! I worked like a slave, saving every cent I could scrape up to give him his education. But now that he's become a big-shot, he couldn't care less about me. What will our relatives say? And what about our friends in the village? I wish I could go off and hide. He doesn't realize what he's done. When you marry, don't do like your brother. Marry a Malay girl."

I thought mother would never stop crying. She kept on crying and sobbing as she listened to father. Maybe it was because she regretted bringing my brother into the world, or perhaps because she hated having a European woman as a daughter-in-law. I don't know which, but I've never seen such sadness in my mother's eyes. Deep regret showed through her wrinkled face. After all, he was her oldest child, the one she had taken so much pride in. Everyone who lived around our small town praised the wisdom my parents used in raising their children. Father himself often bragged about the bright future my brother had before him, "He's already in grade ten of an English medium school, and he will soon graduate. Then he plans to become an officer in the Malaysian army. At the very least he will make a thousand dollars a month."

Mother was not far behind. Every time she would visit a neighbor, or any time someone would come to see her, the subject of conversation would always be the same, "We will soon have to move from the village. Our son wants to live in a big city, and we will go there to live with him. It will be nice not to have to work so hard any more."

But the expected did not happen. What father would not have been angry? What mother would not have wept?

Father did not know it, but I frequently went to visit my brother. Trying to separate us would be like trying to slice water with a knife. It made me really happy to see how successful my brother was; he seemed to be living in luxury. My parents would be lucky to stay in his home. Every time I visited him we talked about the family.

"Is father still angry with me?" my brother once asked, as we were driving around the city in his car.

"Hmm, hmm!" I answered with a nod.

"Angry because I married a European woman?"

Again I nodded.

"Father doesn't understand," my brother added, "and mother doesn't either. None of our relatives back home understand. You and I are the only ones who understand. Isn't a European exactly the same as anyone else, no better and no worse than the rest of us? I am attracted to her. Yes, I love her. But I didn't marry her until she became a Muslim. What's wrong with that? How can that be disgraceful? What does father want? Does he want to choose my wife for me? He's not the one who would have to live with her. How would you like to live with someone you didn't know? Father doesn't understand the changing times. He simply doesn't understand."

All I could do was to nod in agreement. Whenever I was with my brother and listened to him, I was certain that father was at fault. How foolish for anyone in this day and time to hold on to outdated and useless customs; how foolish to discriminate against people whose skin and hair are different from ours. Why was it wrong for my brother to marry the woman he loved? Is it necessary to follow the advice of people who don't really care? It's our life, not theirs. We are the ones who will have to answer for our actions, not them. We have to live with the choices we make, whether good or bad. As I thought about all this, I wanted to rush home as fast as I could and let father in on the way that people look at things nowadays. I wanted to say to him, "Times have changed; things are different now from what they were when you and mother got married. Why make such a fuss about your son's marriage? We don't have to pay attention to what others say. It's none of their business anyhow. We are the ones who will benefit or be hurt. People only know how to laugh. If we laugh, they laugh; but if we cry, they still go on laughing. Father! It's not our place to choose a wife for your son, or to decide on who our in-laws will be. We should be concerned only about his happiness. Is he happy with his wife? Do they enjoy living together? Do they get along with one another? These days it's not up to the family to chose a man's wife, or even her nationality or the color of her skin."

But would father be willing to listen to me? My brother knew what he was talking about—father simply didn't understand. Mother couldn't understand it all either. Moreover, father wouldn't be willing to follow my advice; he's ignorant of changes in the modern world. As far as he's concerned, marriage is for the sake of assuring that the family line continues; and whether the succeeding generations will be good or bad is determined by their ancestors. Father would never change his mind, not even if commanded to do so by an angel from heaven. I knew this for certain.

My brother and his wife were getting along nicely. They had not been separated from one another since his return from Sandhurst four years ago. He was now a captain; but I could still recall the time several years ago when our family sent him off to England. My father, and my mother, and I made a big effort to go to Kuala Lumpur to tell him good-bye. I saw my father crying.

"Take good care of yourself," he said, hugging my brother, "and always keep God in your thoughts."

Mother cried all the while. As I recall, I was sad too; but I knew that though my parents were sobbing, they were as proud as they could be. Success for my brother meant success for them too. A few days later father received a letter from my brother, indicating that he had arrived safely in a place called Eton Hall. I read the letter out loud to my father.

Among other things the letter said, "I arrived safely. Please pray for God to watch over me." Afterwards I noticed that when my parents had finished their prayers, they would often hold their open hands upward. Father folded the letter carefully and placed it in his shirt pocket.

My brother's second letter contained nothing startling. It came while he was training at Sandhurst, the largest military academy in England. My parent's faces were all aglow; every chance they got, they talked about how fortunate their son was. Sometimes mother let herself be carried away, bragging about her son overseas. Father and mother were overcome with joy.

The third letter was addressed to me. In it he mentioned briefly his love for the woman who later was to become his wife. As it turned out, the story was a long one. At that time I myself had become old enough to enjoy dating. My brother made me promise not to say anything to our parents about what he had written.

Finally, I did tell mother, but not father. She sighed deeply; she became sick at heart and gave up all hope. "Have you told your father?" mother asked between sobs.

"Not yet," I replied, saying as few words as possible.

"Don't tell him. Whatever you do, don't tell him." she insisted. "He would run amuk. I'm certain he would."

I honored mother's request, but later on father found out. My brother wrote him a letter, and I was the one who had to read it to him.

"Read us your brother's letter," father said. He was excited; I could see signs of fear and anxiety on mother's face.

I never had the chance to finish. Father became furious and interrupted. "Give me that letter!" he commanded angrily. Then he tore it to bits and threw the pieces on the ground.

"That damned son of mine!" Father shouted. "Who told him to get married? Who said he should marry that heathen woman? Damn his hide!"

Then tears fell from father's eyes; how terribly disappointed he was. Mother went on moaning and moaning. That letter was the beginning of the breach between my father and my brother. For a long time after that father did not ask about him.

A few days later mother said to me, "Tell your brother to divorce that woman. Write him as soon as you can—tell him to leave her." But before I had a chance to write, we received another letter from him, informing us that he would be coming home the following week, and asking the three of us to meet him at the airport. I didn't know what to do. What would happen if he brought his wife home with him to meet father? Moreover, our village was rich only with poverty. How could a European be expected to feel at home there? I remembered all that had happened when we received news of the marriage, and I felt like taking up for father. My brother was thinking of no one but himself. Maybe it didn't seem like much to him, but the sort of thing he had done wouldn't sit well with the people in our village. Everyone would frown down on our family. Yes, my brother was thinking only of himself; he didn't give much thought to the bitter harvest our family would reap. People would try to avoid my parents. Visitors would stop dropping in. We would no longer be invited to the feasts and celebrations. Everywhere people would gossip about my father and mother and their European daughter-in-law. They would be regarded as uncouth as a pair of apes fresh from the jungle. All this because of a hardheaded brother who never gave a thought except to himself. Sure, he was free to do as he pleased, but we should always consider the possible consequences of our actions. It's never right to act foolishly in the name of freedom. We should always be conscious that deeds which profit us individually may also involve our parents and our relatives, and even our entire village or nation.

I was the only one there at the airport to greet my brother. Father and mother wouldn't even talk about it. My brother should certainly understand how our family and relatives felt about his marriage. I was confident that he would feel sorry enough to hurry home and ask father's forgiveness. That would put our family at peace again. I felt relieved.

But nothing happened as I expected. I explained to my brother the reason our parents felt the way they did about his marriage.

"Okay, let them be angry," he replied.

My brother didn't return home with me. A few months later we received a letter from him; he was living in the town of Mentakab in Pahang State. He expressed his disappointment that his parents had not been at the airport to welcome him home. I thought father would have a change of heart when I showed him the letter, but that effort was fruitless too.

"Don't try to talk me into letting your brother return home with that woman of his," father told me, "I don't want the likes of him in this house."

After that, I gave up all hopes of reconciling my father and brother. My parents stayed on in the village, while my brother and his wife remained in Pahang. As for me, I went to work in the city where I enjoyed the life of a bachelor.

But anyone would feel frustrated with a division in the family, especially if the split is between the father whom you love and a brother, who is your own flesh and blood. Besides that, father was growing older day by day. I was completely bewildered.

For almost a year father didn't as much as mention my brother's name; and he had no idea of his daughter-in-law's name. Whenever I had enough time off from work I went to visit my brother. One day, quite unexpectedly, I received a letter from father (I can't imagine who wrote it for him), asking me to come home immediately. So I rushed home.

"Is there any word of your brother?" father inquired after dinner that evening. Mother was sitting there too.

"It's been two months since I've heard from him," I answered.

"Tomorrow write and tell him that he can keep his wife, that I'm not mad at him any longer. But he must take another wife, a Malay. He will never have any children by the wife he has now; and I'm already an old man, and his mother is old too. We want to see a grandchild before we die. We'll never be happy until we do." Father had finished his say.

It occurred to me that perhaps father had changed his mind—that he no longer cared who his daughter-in-law happened to be, or what nationality she was, or anything else. All he wanted was a grandchild. But could my brother's wife have a child? There were no indications that she could; evidently it was impossible for her to have any children. My brother would have to take a second wife. He could afford it on his income, and it was the least he could do for father. Perhaps in this way father would have the opportunity to kiss his grandchild before becoming too decrepit with age.

"Okay, father," I replied. "I'll write him tomorrow." Among other things my letter said:

Please forgive me for waiting so long to write. All three of us are doing fine, and we wish the same for you and your wife. Apparently father is no longer angry with you because of your marriage. I'm grateful for that and happy too. Father told me that he and mother are very lonely these days, but a grandchild would brighten up their lives. Father wants very much to see a grandchild before he dies, and he is concerned because your wife has had no children. How will you feel when you are old and have no children? I think father is right— life without children is no better than being an orphan. Father would like for you to take a second wife. Surely you don't object to that, and

*perhaps you could then have a child. Father and mother would be so
relieved; they won't be with us much longer, and it would be good if
we could fulfill their wishes during their last days.*

That is some of what was in the letter. I thought the breach would
finally be healed. My brother would give the matter much thought
and then do as father had requested. Gradually I began to feel better
about the entire situation.

A week later we received a reply, indicating that my brother would
do all he could to satisfy father's wishes. He would take a second
wife, just to please father. That same day I went to the village to give
the news to father and mother. I've never seen such a big smile on
father's face. Most likely he was having visions of a beautiful little
chubby grandchild. Mother couldn't stop laughing. They had
wanted a grandchild for so long. My only wish was that his next wife
would be Malay, and that she could have children. If not, my parents
would be more disappointed than ever.

I waited for a letter from my brother. I felt certain that he would
mention his future bride's name and inform us of the wedding date.
Father was eager to have the wedding according to Malay custom—
the ritual of asking for the bride's hand in marriage, the engagement
ceremony, the exchange of gifts, the wedding itself, and the reading
of the Quran.

When I read my brother's next letter, I was shocked out of my
senses. He was not going to take a second wife.

*Your sister-in-law has done nothing wrong. She is a good and
faithful wife, and I'm happy with her. Why should I punish one of
God's people when she has not sinned? Please explain this to father,
and tell him that I beg his forgiveness. But in order to make him and
mother happy, I now have a child—an adopted one. The baby's
mother is Chinese, and we were able to get the baby at a real bargain
price; all we had to pay was a hundred dollars. It's a boy; and we've
named him Hassan. I will let father and mother raise the boy. They
will be thrilled to have a grandchild, even though he is an adopted
child. Please let me know when they would like for me to bring him to
them.*

The letter really upset me. My brother was cruel and heartless, and
my parents would be heartbroken to hear the news. What would it

do to father to hear that his son had bought him a Chinese grandchild for a hundred dollars?

My first thought was to keep silent about the letter. But it would not be fair to make father go on waiting for news about a second marriage which was never going to take place. I had to tell him.

"What! He bought a Chinese boy?" father yelled, after I read him the letter. "Oh God! My God, my God! Help this stupid son of mine!" Then father buried his face in his pillow. That was the first time in all my life that I had seen father cry like that; he wept like a child who had been punished for doing something wrong. Mother ran into her room, but I could hear her loud sobs. And before I realized what was happening, tears flowed down from my own eyes. How could my brother be so cruel? My blood began to boil. Is this any way for a son to treat his parents?

The wound which had almost healed was opened again. But this time it would go from bad to worse; it would fester and spread. The dawning day had suddenly turned to darkness.

Although in my own thinking the adoption of the child was not as bad as had been imagined by my parents, it nevertheless left an indelible scar on them. I blamed my brother for what had happened, and so I refused any longer to try and coax him to please our parents. Never again would I attempt to talk sense into a stubborn fool like him. Let him keep as far away from our family as he could. Let him live his own life. But I realized also that something had to be done as quickly as possible to heal the wound in my father's heart. No one else in the whole world could do it except me, the youngest child.

That same month I informed my parents of my desire to get married; they were delighted beyond measure. All the arrangements and plans were hurriedly made for the wedding and the dinner. Before the year was out the wedding took place. Father slaughtered a large bull, and mother busied herself making all the necessary preparations. My parents' faces glowed with delight as I took the wedding vows. Father had forbidden us to invite my brother.

By God's grace, later that same month my wife began to vomit and have headaches. Two months later she began craving unripe mangoes. Exactly ten months after our wedding she gave birth to a daughter. I can still see father holding the baby in his lap after its bath and rubbing his nose against its rosey cheeks. Then he placed the baby in mother's lap, and they took turns kissing it.

Life in this world is no longer without meaning for my parents—they have both lived to see their grandchild.

 *Born in 1933, Shahnon Ahmad is regarded by many critics as the top fiction writer in Malaysia today. He is also dean at a Malaysian university. Mr. Ahmad writes short stories, poetry, novels, essays and literary criticism. Some of his work has been translated into English, Danish, Dutch and Russian. He has been awarded many National Literary Awards; he was one of six recipients of the Literary Pioneer Prizes in 1976 for his untiring efforts in literature. The story was translated by Barclay M. Newman.*

"I don't understand us . . .
We are angels and fiends almost
in the same thought."

The Hunted Hare

BY EDITH CAMPION

**"Each outcry of the hunted hare
a fibre from the brain does tear."**

MR. Meadows pressed his lips together and sighed sadly as the sheep truck overtook and passed his sober VW beetle. He was not sighing because of being overtaken. He was quite used to being passed traveling at his lawful fifty miles an hour. No—he was sighing for the poor creatures with their white guileless faces, swaying in the truck that carried them to their death. He could see they knew this was no ordinary journey.

Mr. Meadows was a devout vegetarian. He tried neither to eat nor wear anything that had come, as it were, from "the stricken deer." He was a very hesitant man. Not because he lacked substance in word or thought but because he was very aware how hurtful words could be when used indiscriminately. The result was rather that of speaking with a stammerer. People waited, not for the broken words but for Mr. Meadows to sift his thoughts and make absolutely sure that they contained no hidden venom.

Everything called to him. Man, woman, child. The beasts of the field and jungle. The fowls of the air and the fish of the deep. He was exhausted by their despair, their need.

The morning paper began the martyrdom of his day. He drank his tea and clacked his tongue at each disaster, each uncaring action. He was sorry for the unborn child but equally distressed for the woman forced to carry an unwanted child and then support it, perhaps unwillingly, for 21 years or more. He felt deeply for the death of native trees, yet he would not wish the careless axeman to want for money or food. He was a battlefield of the heart without victory or defeat. The sorrows and cares of the world lay heavy upon him. Each night he fell into bed exhausted, spent.

His work days were filled with thoughts of—"how tired Mrs. Bracey looks" and—"has Miss Philipps been crying again?" Sometimes, at a tea break, he would find himself asked what he felt or thought of this or that situation, which would cause a storm in his mind because he was completely open-ended. He could see each person's difficulties with equal weight so he could never say that the scales came down more heavily on one side or the other.

"What do you honestly think of him?" Miss Philipps asked Mrs. Bracey. "Is he nuts?"

"No—actually he's just too kind, too ready to see the burdens people carry."

"Well, I think he's nuts, and so does Harry."

"Harry's great on the football field but I wouldn't give him ten out of ten for perception or sensitivity."

"He's no fool."

"Of course not, dear." And she turned away from Kay Philipps with a maddening Mona Lisa smile on her lips.

Mr. Meadows was a member of every organization which catered for the needy—human or animal. Amnesty International was perhaps the cause which taxed him beyond emotional bearing. He could read the *Newsletter* only section by section. He would have drowned had he exposed himself to the whole in one sitting. All that human misery—man's inhumanity to man. He would start letters to States and Countries, beseeching mercy for "Prisoners of the Month" and as he read their case histories of imminent executions, he would rise to his feet, and leaving the unfinished letter, he would walk about his room asking his bookcase, his mirror and the black and white horses caught in a thunderstorm, their minds fear-riven: "What in the name of God is the human race coming to?" And he would stand still, his head raised as if waiting for an answer from the Heavenly Father.

His concern for the universe crammed his nights with harsh, cruel dreams which tossed him in his bed and filled the dark room with his mumbled broken protests.

He would wake without the balm of easeful sleep and some mornings he would rise early and in the gathering light, he would walk to an adjacent park, climb its promontory and feeling like Moses, watch the sun drag itself from the east. The splendor of the morning would occasionally evoke temporary optimism, "God's in His Heaven, all's right with the world," which would almost immediately be dissipated by the scream of a fire siren or the distant wail of an ambulance. Mr. Meadows would walk from the park, talking in his mind to himself and to God.

Age had advanced, as age invariably does, the anguish of Mr. Meadow's futile care for his fellow creatures. With this growth he became careless of self. He forgot the small duties that make one acceptable to one's own kind. Clean linen was the first to go. Shaving and washing were sometimes omitted and there was often no food in the house. He now started to talk openly to God. As he ambled along the street, he would pause by a lamppost: "How can you allow it?" he would question. "How can you permit the use of such weapons?" And shaking his head he would continue on his way to work, pleading and admonishing his unanswering deity.

Mrs. Bracey watched the fall of her angel with concern. She marked that he no longer carried a lunch to work and increased her own package to share with him.

Miss Philipps hissed in Mrs. Bracey's ear with satisfaction: "Didn't I tell you? Didn't Harry know? He's nuts!"

"Well, he's a very wholesome nut."

"Not down wind!" And having added another nail to Mr. Meadow's coffin, she dispersed—vanished back to her desk with its odd assortment of objets plastiques that included a tiny nun of

Japanese manufacture set in a plastic cylinder, a tile with a kewpie-like figure wearing an apron, displaying a message—"love is . . . cleaning up your old mess before making a new mess," a photo of Harry in a heart-shaped frame and some tiny flowers of the everlasting variety.

Mrs. Bracey decided to tackle Mr. Meadows over a shared lunch.

"Shall we eat in the rose garden?"

"You're very kind, Mrs. Bracey."

And they walked up the hill into the square of full blown and tight budded flowers standing proud upon their barbed stems.

"Beautiful," said Mr. Meadows stooping to take the breath of a buxom red. "Some things remain beautiful, in spite of everything."

"Yes," said Mrs. Bracey as she unscrewed the thermos. "Some things remain beautiful."

She unwrapped the sandwiches. The noise of an aircraft disturbed Mr. Meadows. Lifting his eyes to the sky, he watched the jet with its comet-like tail.

"Now that's beautiful too, but it can also be dark and destructive." And his mind filled with a rain of black bullets falling from the sky, enlarging in descent to huge dark cones of death. He sighed: "I don't understand us, Mrs. Bracey. We are angels and fiends almost in the same thought."

"Do have your tea." She handed the cup and observed the delicate, dirt-ingrained hand with its chipped nails. "Mr. Meadows—" she hesitated and resolutely drew in her breath. "Mr. Meadows, you must stop carrying the cares of the world." She handed him a sandwich. "No man is strong enough. I doubt if God is strong enough." He didn't reply. "At least reduce your care, restrict it to smaller areas where it may be possible to achieve some small success."

He sucked at the hot tea.

"I think you're right. . . . I believe you are right, Mrs. Bracey. But. . . ." His hand was trembling. ". . . I don't seem able to cut myself free. It's as if I'm joined—shackled—to God and His concerns. He needs me." He bit into the sandwich. "And I don't feel it's right to leave Him alone with such a plateful of trouble."

"But, Mr. Meadows, if you continue like this you will certainly lose your job—it's only a matter of time."

He sighed heavily and returned the cup.

"I suppose you're right. I haven't given it proper thought. I've been thinking of other things." And his eye was attracted to a pretty youngster of six or seven. "Take that child, Mrs. Bracey—pretty, young and free. But what will life do to her? Will she be cheated and perhaps destroyed?"

"Look! You must take a pull on yourself. No one can afford to be taken over by such negative forces—not everything ends in tears." She looked at her watch. "I'm very fond of you, Mr. Meadows. I want to help."

"The trouble is I'm sort of committed—committed to take a little weight for Him." He cast his eyes skyward. "If I can sort things out a bit, for Him, perhaps I may then opt out of the picture."

Mrs. Bracey felt a surge of irritation, which was immediately vanquished when she looked into the guileless, unshaven face with the evasive, apologetic blue eyes.

"I've distressed you," he was very humble. "And you are always kind. Let me get rid of the rubbish."

They walked back to the office in silence. Mr. Meadows was in private conference with God on the speed of traffic and the vulnerability of the human form. As they reached the office building Mrs. Bracey turned to him:

"Look—please try—please allow me to help."

"You're very kind—and if you can help us, I'll call on you." Mrs. Bracey sighed, acknowledging defeat.

That evening Mr. Meadows walked home, an untidy, derelict figure arguing passionately at lampposts as he passed them. "However," he said, allowing the stream of people to break and surge on either side of him, "—she's a fine, generous and compassionate woman." Heads turned back to look at the shabby man with his wooden companion.

That night God spoke to Mr. Meadows as he slept. "Let us work together wholeheartedly, that the crooked may be made straight."

Next morning Mr. Meadows did not go to work and he and God got down to it, face to face, with elbows on the kitchen table.

They outlawed killing, torture, poverty. In the afternoon they took the air in the park. It was wonderful to have a companion, a fellow crusader. Sitting on a bench they dealt, in more desultory way with the *petits suisses* of human and animal behavior.

"You see," said Mr. Meadows, "—smart witty talk is often full of wounding barbs."

A woman pushing a pram with a toddler attached to the handle, glanced in surprise at the grubby, untidy man as he chatted happily to himself. He caught her eyes, and smiled. She smiled back. His was the purest, most open greeting she had received in weeks.

"Well, I must be getting home." And he took his leave of God, for the day.

After an absence of nine days from the office, Mrs. Bracey became concerned for Mr. Meadows and saw the manager.

"He's a very good man," she explained. "But I fear the troubles of the world have taken him over."

"What can we do?"

"Well, I realize he's no longer much use at his job, but I'm not sure if he has any close friends or relatives. If something isn't done he may easily starve to death."

"How about welfare?"

"They may help. But honestly, he's not dangerous. I can't think of anyone else who is so free of malice."

In good time, mainly unhurried time, the welfare officer knocked on Mr. Meadows' door. He acknowledged the uncut grass and the tumble of weeds and flowers. The door opened and a lightly bearded man of late middle years greeted him.

"Come in. Come in." The house was a shambles.

"Thank you." Mr. Meadows led him to the kitchen.

"Sit down. Sit down—no, not that one—that's His."

The young man took another chair looking carefully at the empty place which was "His."

"Who is your friend, Mr. Meadows?"

"That's Mr. G. We work together."

"I've come because the people at your place of work were worried about you—thought you might be ill."

"Oh, no, no—no. It's just that Mr. G and I have important business. I'll return when it is concluded."

Jim Parker took an eye-voyage of the untidy kitchen which was festooned in open and discarded pages of newspaper. The table was heavily crumbed with patches on the cloth where jam had bled. Unwashed pots stood at ease on the stove and dirty dishes had pyramided above the sink-top.

The table contained no food except two small broken pieces of bread whose pores had opened as they gave up their moisture.

"I'm afraid I'm out of tea and coffee." Mr. Meadows thought hard. "Perhaps I could make some mint tea—I—have some growing—somewhere—"

"No, please. Don't trouble. As I said, I called because the people at your place of work were worried. Are you ill?"

"No. No! No—just a little tired. We have so much work to do, so many things to discuss—there's simply not enough time in the day."

He's uncomfortably thin, thought Jim Parker.

"Do you receive pay for this—er—work?" Mr. Meadows laughed: "If you work with Him, it's on a voluntary basis."

"I see. But how do you manage to eat?" Mr. Meadows nodded.

"That is something of a problem, and it seems unlikely that I shall ever reach His spiritual sufficiency—still there are compensations."

"May I ask the nature of this work?"

"Of course. Of course." He thought deeply, looking at his grubby spread hands. "You see, it's a matter of need. There are voices, calling out. . . begging, demanding succor. They all call out—to me—. My head is like an immense telephone exchange, full of voices." He sighed. "It's a bad business . . . And it's not just our kind. If you listen—really listen—there are the voices of creatures and plants and trees, even the rivers have their sorrow, their pain." He paused.

"What do you—and—" Jim nodded to the empty chair "—hope to achieve?"

"Well, it's a big job. We're slowly sifting our way through—solutions are not obvious but—together we'll find them."

He's a very sweet, harmless old fool, thought Jim, but he must be looked after or he'll starve to death.

"Look," he said. "I have an idea. Suppose I find a place which will provide food and care for you and your friend, leaving you free to continue the good work?"

"Could you?" The question lit a candle in his face. He glowed and relaxed. "That would be a relief—much better to be a full-timer on the job. We're both eternally (he smiled at the word)—grateful."

"Have you any cash?"

Mr. Meadows thought hard.

"Perhaps—" and he stood. "Gray trousers, back pocket." He trotted from the room, returning with five dollars and some change.

"Shall I buy some bread, butter, tea and a few things to see you through until I can make arrangements?"

"You see?" Mr. Meadows addressed the empty chair. "You haven't made such a bad go of it. You mustn't give up. People can be good—can be kind."

He looked into Jim's face.

"We are truly grateful. And now, if you will excuse me, we have work to do." He accompanied Jim to the door and watched his progress down the untidy path to the gate. Jim could hear his voice.

"Nationalism—we must be rid of it. Take away the flags and the guns and the heartless leaders—we must move freely without frontiers—the children. . ." And the door closed upon the heavenly debate.

Jim returned to the house with a large brown paper parcel filled with groceries he hoped would contain Mr. Meadows until the wheels of welfare had ground and placed him in the appropriate institution. He knocked at the door and heard footsteps and the voice advance along the passage. The heavily frosted glass caught and enlarged Mr. Meadows until he swung open the door.

"Oh, how very kind, how thoughtful." He clasped the bag in his arms.

"If you need anything else, I'm sure Mrs. Bracey would be willing to help. I shall be in touch as soon as I discover a working area for you."

"You're very good to us."

"Goodbye."

Jim Parker passed in his report and because he felt somehow engaged, committed to this particular case, he visited his head of department and explained Mr. Meadows as well as he could to his superior.

"So you see, he's a pleasant, harmless old guy, just trying, with God's help to straighten out the world. But in the process, he's likely to starve to death." There was a slight pause.

"I suppose, he may recover—if he can complete the task."

"Not much chance of that," said Alfred Huxley. "He's bitten off a bit more than he can chew. Still, let's look after him while he's busy."

"Would you allow me to escort him? He knows me now, and I do understand his particular fixation."

"How will he settle in?"

"No trouble, I should think. As long as he remains concentrated on the world's woes, he won't have time for personal problems."

The wheels of the Welfare State began to turn.

Two weeks later Jim Parker returned to Mr. Meadows' house. He had tried to telephone to let Mr. Meadows know what had been happening, but the telephone had been disconnected—probably the light and heat were shot too, thought Jim.

Mr. Meadows welcomed him as an old and trusted friend. "We were wondering about you—I said any day now—and here you are! Now, what's to be done? What do we need?"

"I think just a bag of personal clothing, and the odd books, perhaps, that give you pleasure."

Two books were hastily picked from the shelves—a large Bible of comfortable print and the Works of William Blake.

"Nothing else?"

"No. There won't be much time, and these are my favorites."

"And the clothes?"

"Ah. That is a little more difficult." He became evasive. "It's a matter of hygiene. Perhaps after all we can't really travel."

"Do you mean they're soiled, dirty?"

"You might say that. Yes. That, I'm afraid is the case."

"Let me help you. They'll wash them at the place." Jim could not bring himself to name Mr. Meadows' new abode.

"Well, if you don't mind . . ." The state of his clothing had temporarily unhooked Mr. Meadows from *welt weh.* "Follow me." And he led Jim to a musty dark bedroom. "I'm afraid the lights don't work."

The bed was unmade, the white sheets were gray. Again, the newspaper leaves had been shed to create a bloodless autumn. "I'll miss the old place," said Mr. Meadows, rummaging in a drawer and cupboard. "I'm not sure where my case is." A plane passed overhead. "Pity they were ever invented," said Mr. Meadows listening to its whine.

Looking under the bed, Jim discovered an old battered suitcase. It was leather and had seen better days. A few exotic labels still proclaimed their place of origin.

"Did you travel once?"

"No—no. My father and mother did a bit of gadding about." He opened the case and started to thrust in his personal effects, the clean and soiled embraced each other.

"Have you a razor?"

Mr. Meadows felt his beard with surprise.

"Yes. I'll collect the things from the bathroom." He returned with his toilet gear and a hair brush. Some of the spirit had drained out of him. "I know it's for the best, but I've lived here a fair number of years."

"Perhaps you can return when the work's done."

"I suppose you're right, but I feel I'm leaving an old friend in a bad way." And he sat for a moment on the bed with his head bowed. Then he straightened his shoulders against private grief and said: "But the work I'm doing for Him is more important." And he pushed himself from the bed, struggled and finally closed the bulging case. "Ready. We're ready for you."

Jim packed him into the front seat. As the car drew away Mr. Meadows' head turned slowly back towards his old home until it was edged from his sight.

He was silent during the journey and did not register the large iron gates or the name of the institution. He perked up a little on the way up the drive.

"Nice lawns. Good to see some trees and flowers."

He was admitted and became a file among other files. But already his mind was beginning to concentrate on the work which lay ahead. Jim walked with him to the ward. Mr. Meadows was surprised to find his work was to be shared, but he comforted himself with the thought that many minds make light work.

"Well, I suppose this is where I leave you. But I would like to visit you if you would be happy to see me."

"Of course. Of course. It would be a great pleasure—a rest from our labors."

He shook Jim's hand and watched his back disappear. He sat on his bed and raising his head returned to the debate.

"There are still earthquake victims to be sorted out . . . clothes and food . . . something must be done to settle the Jewish-Arab situation . . . again we need an end to nationalism . . . get rid of the flags . . . we must become one people . . . ."

The days became months and the months became years until one especial day as Mr. Meadows walked about the gardens, gesticulating and debating and he took an unexpected jump to another ambiance.

It was as if he were suddenly a captive audience in a television studio. Cards were held up for his responses: *Thou shalt not . . . Love Thy Neighbour . . . To Thine Own Self Be . . . But The Greatest Of These Is Charity . . . .*

"Yes. Yes!" Mr. Meadows nodded his head enthusiastically at the last card. "But," he paused. "On the other hand—" He looked up to God's gray sky. "All things considered . . . to begin again?"

He stood with his hands clasped, his head to one side, his mouth happily ajar.

"Pull the plug, eh? Why not pull the plug on the whole messy business? Start afresh . . . well, that's my thinking . . . that's my considered opinion. And you can't say I haven't given it time and thought. That's the best, the very best, advice I can give . . . from now on, You're on Your own. I've done all I can—I'm finished. It's over and out for me. Go ahead. Pull the plug!"

He turned, clasped his hands behind his back and tapping the knuckles of one hand upon the palm of the other, walked jauntily away from the somber brick building which had become his home.

Born in 1923 in Wellington, Edith Campion attended the Queen Margaret and Nga Tawa schools. At the age of 13 she "escaped" on a pony in the dead of night from Nga Tawa. Her education continued "privately, oddly, and splendidly." She and her husband trained at the Old Vic Theater School, London, and founded a touring company on their return to New Zealand. Mrs. Campion started to write seriously in 1971.

"Her disappointment,
her quite unjustified disappointment,
hangs in the air like a grievance . . ."

The Child

BY CORA SANDEL

A marriage not made in Heaven.

IT could have been a corner of paradise, but instead it was something quite different. Who would have guessed that it looked like
this? In a corner of the sofa there is a doll, its bright, black, beady
eyes staring straight ahead.

There are flowering plants on the window sill, fuchsia and
geranium, in full bloom. The curtains are of light, filmy material.
They flutter in the summer breeze. A couple of windows are open,
the panes bright and clear. Books are lying on the table, others are
on shelves around the room. Many books on varied subjects.
About life and death and love, in verse and prose. A piece of
embroidery lies about, a delicate, feminine trifle of fine lace and
thin silk, soft as the skin of a child.

The piano is open. Choice music, both old and modern, stands
open on the music rest: Chopin, Scriabin.

A child may come through the door, trip across the floor, take the doll in its arms and prattle to it; search among the books on the table for one with pictures, dab with one finger at the piano. A fresh, healthy child, with bare arms and legs, tanned by sun and wind, grubby in a clean way as children are from rolling in sand and grass, paddling on the beach, making mud-pies or dandelion chains, eating chocolate.

Its eyes are those of a happy child, open and carefree, as yet unaware of its environment.

Grown-ups also have their life here. But they know where they stand.

The woman goes in and out. She waters the flowers, tidies up, dusts, sits down occasionally with a book, or with the embroidery which lies there, sewing a stitch or two, never many. Some embroideries are never finished and this is such a one. There are also books which are only glanced at, never read. They lie there mute; time and again they are slammed shut and tossed aside.

She is restless. Hardly has she sat down before she is up again, finding something to do here and there; polishing a window pane already bright, rubbing a polished surface with the duster, occupying herself with many an unnecessary task. Occasionally she hums. But she also wipes away a stray tear appearing suddenly in the corner of her eye on its way down her cheek. She is slim and dark.

She may come in with her hands all wet, an expression of longing on her face. Abruptly she wipes her hands on her apron and dashes to the piano. Drama follows. Two voices seem to be skirmishing, one sneering and scornful, the other pursuing with appeal, with threat; they meet in a wild clash, in pain and joy.

Suddenly the music becomes a jarring discord. She lets both hands fall onto the keyboard so that the instrument wails loudly: she bends forward, her head touching the keys and the piano wails again. Tears fall between her fingers.

But she can also play a nocturne as gently as if it were night and someone had to be soothed to sleep; it brings a little moisture to her cheeks.

She may get up and waltz in the middle of the floor. She may also move from one side of the room to the other with long, soundless steps like an animal in a cage. Always in the end her handkerchief is called into use.

She hears the child coming, wipes her face quickly and changes her expression like an experienced actress. The child comes bounding in, leaving the door open, and topples headlong into its mother's arms, crying or laughing as small children will. Or it may bring her flowers, a posy made up of all kinds of wild flowers, some with short stalks, others with long, quite unsuitable for the vases that nevertheless receive them. Look, there they are, don't they look beautiful!

Another time the child may have grazed itself and holds out a small, grubby fist, or shows a rounded knee covered in sand and bearing traces of blood. It whimpers, calls for mother. It must be helped and comforted and no one is more easily comforted. Soon the child laughs again; it sits on the sofa with the doll in its arms and a bandage around the wound, sucking something nice and looking into the picture book. The mother talks and laughs with it, keeps it occupied, takes it into her arms again and again, and kisses it. It is as if there is a grain of self-reproach, of apprehension in her manner. She sings snatches of songs, tells fairy tales. "Once upon a time there was a tiny, wee, little woman, who lived in a tiny, wee, little house—"

The child listens with shining eyes, full of anticipation. But suddenly the mother loses the thread and cannot find it again. Preoccupied and irritable, she pushes the child down from her lap: "There, now, you must go out again and play. We can't sit in here all day."

And the child goes without question. That is what usually happens. It has happened many times.

Towards evening the mother hears the click of the garden gate, and the sound of a man's footsteps on the gravel path. Her restless face at once becomes closed and taut.

She moves hurriedly round the room closing the piano, putting away the music, covering up her traces. For a moment she stands with the embroidery in her hands, uncertain, but leaves it lying on the table.

Then she goes out of the room.

The husband comes in.

He is what one would call a decent man, correct, inspiring confidence, well-groomed, in his prime. Without doubt he is also pleasant and companionable, and should be able to look forward to peace and quiet in his home, but he cannot. He looks round with misgiving, biting his lips, muttering to himself.

The child has come in with him. There it stands leaning against his knee, full of the day's adventures. It has seen a squirrel, such a sweet, little squirrel. It has seen a hedgehog, such a sweet, little hedgehog. It has plucked a nice posy for mother, there it is.

Yes, isn't it nice!

The father takes the child on his lap, but his thoughts are elsewhere.

The child demands his attention. It picks up the picture book and sits pointing. The father says mechanically: "Yes, what a nice pussycat. Yes, what a fine cockadoodledoo."

His eyes are on the door, he listens. And suddenly he pushes the child off his lap and picks up the telephone; he quickly dials a number and is in the middle of a conversation when the mother enters.

He neither sees nor hears her, he laughs and talks animatedly, as a man fully occupied with his friends and pleasures. Not even when he has replaced the receiver does he appear to remember her but remains there looking up more numbers in the telephone book, more distractions.

"Good evening," she says lightly and sits down.

"Oh, there you are. Good evening."

"Well—?"

Her voice is impatient but also full of childish expectation: but she is disappointed. He shrugs his shoulders: "Well—no—nothing special."

There she sits as if she had expected to hear something out of the ordinary. She is always waiting for this husband of hers to say something that he never says; all her married life she has been waiting. She is not quite sure exactly what she is waiting for, she only knows that to-night is another disappointment.

"No—," he gestures vaguely with empty hands.

His day has been exactly like all other days. Nothing has happened. He comes home from the same routine as yesterday and the day before, and he is not a man of imagination to whom the gray everyday becomes charged with adventure. He is not a creature of moods either, one whose feelings ebb and flow, with unexpected outbursts. Instinctively, he plays as well as he can the part of being a deep nature, someone of whom one cannot be quite sure, telephoning to so-called friends, and so on. But the part does not suit him, he is not good at it, and he does not like playing it. It is natural to him to be open and frank.

But the part he plays does not help matters. She still sits there, antagonistic and unreasonable. Her disappointment, her quite unjustified disappointment, hangs in the air like a grievance, causing him to be even more taciturn than is his nature. What the deuce is it she wants?

"Well, and how about you?" His lips curl ironically.

"All right, thank you," she replies, also ironically.

Anxious to disperse the feeling of grievance in the air, he walks straight into trouble. He picks up the embroidery, handles it clumsily and says: "You've got to be a woman to have time and patience for this kind of thing."

"Time! Good heavens, it has been lying here for weeks: if only I had time—"

She stops. Exasperated, he looks about the room, at the piano. It is closed, there is no music to be seen. He has come up against the Great Wall, the insurmountable, the all-absorbing task of running a house, demanding sacrifices surpassing all understanding. For a moment he is at a loss.

But he recovers and returns to the embroidery as a likely starting point for a fresh sortie: "I don't think I have seen this before."

"There are one or two things you don't see," she says as she gets up: "Now it is time to eat."

At the same time she bursts into a loud, scornful laugh, too loud.

"Think of the—," he makes signs, reproachfully, with his head towards the child, which has looked up in surprise.

"I think of nothing else. If I did—"

"If you did—?" He looks at her provokingly.

"Oh!"

Taking the child by the hand, she leaves the room: "Come on, shall we two go and wash our hands."

The meal is, surprisingly, homely, well-cooked, everyday food. Fried mackerel, new potatoes, salad, half a bottle of beer and a sweet. It should taste good.

And to him it does taste good, at least to begin with. He thinks there is a truce. "This tastes good," he says, appreciatively.

"Does it?" she counters coldly. "I'm glad to hear it."

After that they both speak to the child. Quite mechanically they say such things as grown-ups always say to children.

"What have you been doing all day?"

"The right hand, my pet."

"Have you been playing with the other children?"

"Naughty, naughty, look how you've spilt on mother's clean cloth! You mustn't hold your spoon like that—like this."

"And the chicks next door? How are they?"

"You mustn't only eat potatoes. Eat up your fish. That's better."

The child answers to right and left, is quite pleased to be the center of so much attention; it has no idea that this is dangerous ground; doesn't see the wide open pitfalls.

A cat has taken a chick. Another one was trodden on by its mother; she knew no better, poor thing. It broke its leg and had to be killed; they had to kill the sweet, little chick. But now it is buried and there is a cross on the grave, and a peony. And fish is not nice when you're not hungry.

The child twists and turns in its chair and refuses to eat any more fish. The parents continue skirmishing across the child.

"Well, leave it then, my pet."

"Eat it up nicely now."

"Perhaps your portion was too big. Perhaps there was too much for you."

"No more fuss, child. Be good and eat it up or you won't have any sweet."

The child says that it can eat the sweet, but not the fish. It leans backward in its chair and begins to bang the spoon on the plate. It does not sit properly at table and the mother is going to send it away without any sweet.

But the father fetches the sweet himself from the sideboard, sprinkles sugar on it and puts it before the child: "We won't say another word about it. We mustn't ask too much in this summer heat. We should make allowances."

Well, for once he has behaved like the master of the house. He has also managed to impart a double meaning. That pleases him.

The child starts eating the sweet. But it looks from one to the other, disturbed, shy. There comes the first faint realization that life is not always smooth.

The parents do not speak another word.

The evening has come. A summer evening with the heavy foliage still and dark against a sky as brittle and as clear as glass, but all the time getting darker until first one then another star appears. There is a scent of hay, of clover and roses. In the grass somewhere is a tireless siskin. The scenery is more than ever like paradise.

In the room where the piano stands the ceiling light has been lit. The night-moths tumble against the closed windows. Through the open windows some of them come flying in, attracted by the light, and cannot find their way out again; they continue to whirl around and around against the soft lamp-shade. They can be seen behind it like helpless, stupid, small shadows.

He is sitting in here.

He has put away the paper and sits watching the night-moths. It is useless trying to help them. You can only let them persevere until death takes pity on them. But he knows how they feel. He himself flew into the light once and there is the deuce of a difference between being inside, and looking in from the outside. One thinks one has found a warm embrace, a bosom on which to rest; sweetness, peace. But instead one has found a persistent antagonist, capricious, incomprehensible. Music? Not a note. The piano stands silent, a symbol of grievance, of accusation against him. If he did not long so terribly for companionship with her, his child's mother, he would leave and go far away.

From the garden he can hear her footsteps. Out there she wanders.

She walks and walks, the gravel crunches under her feet. Now and then she stops and then the stillness becomes so charged with things left unsaid, things he cannot even guess at, that he moves uneasily in his chair.

She, too, sees the night-moths, she too thinks of the attraction of the light. She herself flew into something she believed would be everlasting adventure, ecstasy without end. She goes there consumed with longing for new and ever new meanings of one single, eternal thing with longing for him, the father of her child. She is rent with longing for this strange man whom she believes is sitting in there reading his paper completely unruffled, and with resentment at his everlasting imperturbability.

The child is asleep on its small, white cot. It has kicked off the bedclothes because of the heat and lies there with bare, brown, chubby limbs, its face like a flower. The child is far away in a dream, has forgotten the pangs of a new and inexplicable pain which for only a second cut through it. It is unaware that it forms the living link of flesh and blood and nerves which binds together two incompatible human beings and that for this it will be made to suffer. In the fullness of time.

Cora Sandel (pen name of Sara Margreth Fabricius) was introduced in SSI No. 3 with her story "Flight to America." Her novel Kranes Konditori *broke all selling record in Norway where it was made into a movie. Lydia Cranfield translated the story.*

"Does the Codger know she hasn't
come back alone?"

The Codger

BY MARIA NUROWSKA

**Neighbors' anguish in anticipation of a father's greeting for
his wayward daughter.**

HE sang as he walked along. People stopped. They stared.

He's singing, they said.

Where's he going?

They say Heddi's come back.

Heddi's back? And the Codger knows?

Yes, he's going to the station to fetch her.

What exactly does he know?

They told him Heddi was back. He put on his coat and is going to
the station to fetch her.

He's taken his cap off. His gray hair's falling down over his eyes
and he's walking along singing.

What did they tell the Codger about Heddi's arrival?

Oh, that she's back. That she's waiting at the station.

He took his coat off the peg without a word and now he's on his
way.

When a girl was born to the Codger he named her after the Headman's wife.

The Headman went to the inn and knocked it back. Afterwards he stopped outside the Codger's house. The Codger came out and leant against the fence.

"You named the girl Hedwig?" asked the Headman.

"That I did," replied the Codger.

The Headman turned on his heel and went off. He mounted a horse, but did not ride far. Afterwards it was a long time before he could lower his feet off the bed.

In the spring everyone knew that the Codger was going to call on the Headman. The Headman's wife cleared the table and brought out a bottle. The Headman dragged himself out of bed, and they sat down on the bench.

Says the Old Man:

"Let's drink, because I no longer feel a grudge against you. You have your Hedwig, I have mine. Let's bury the hatchet and be friends again."

But Heddi hasn't come back alone. Does the Codger know she hasn't come back alone?

He doesn't seem to, or he wouldn't be walking along singing like that. And walking and singing is what he's doing.

The Codger must be headed off. Go and see the Headman and have him think up some way of heading off the Codger, or else when the Old Man sees that Heddi hasn't come back alone he'll kill her.

There's nothing for it but to rush over to the Headman's house and have him get on his bicycle and set off after the Old Man. He's simply got to make it in time, because the Codger will kill Heiddi.

The Headman gets on his bicycle. He's swearing blue murder because there was a christening at the Witeks' yesterday and the Headman knocked it back. The Headman's eyes are all but popping out of his skull from pain. The Headman curses Heddi for choosing to come back just when there was a christening at the Witeks'. He curses the Codger for going to fetch her and having no idea that Heddi hasn't come back alone. He curses the bicycle for refusing to travel on sand.

The time that a tree fell on the Headman and they took him to hospital tongues began to wag that the Szymon boy was hanging around the Headman's Hedwig. The Codger called on the Headman's wife. Without a word he unbuckled his belt and larruped the woman on her bare backside.

After that Hedwig never let the Szymon boy in again.

The Codger's reached the top of the hill. From there the station buildings can be seen. The Codger reached the top of the hill and the Headman may not be in time because his chain has come off. The Headman has to abandon his bicycle and walk the rest of the way on foot.

A cart and horses must be fetched and the Headman given a lift or he won't be in time.

But all the horses are out in the fields.

No, there's a mare in Szymon's stable because she's cast a shoe. Szymon was meaning to go to the Blacksmith, but he knocked it back at the Witeks' christening and now he's sleeping it off in the loft.

"Wake Szymon up! Tell him to hitch up the mare and give the Headman a lift, or else the Headman won't catch up the Codger who's already reached the top of hill from which the station buildings can be seen.

The Headman and the Codger were in the army together. When the Codger caught a bullet, the Headman carried him six miles on his back.

They came back to the village. Both of them called on the beautiful Hedwig. They met outside her house.

"She's mine!" said the Headman and barred the Codger's way.

"Out of my way!" said the Codger.

But eventually—nobody knows why—the Codger turned back and the Headman was left with the field to himself.

Cursing, the Headman is trudging up the hill, Szymon is clambering down from the loft and the Codger has stopped and, shielding his eyes, is gazing down at the station.

The Codger's standing on the top of the hill and scanning the station for a glimpse of Heddi.

Szymon had better hurry getting down from his loft.

Go on, at that distance the Codger won't see anything, not well enough at any rate to make out whether Heddi's come back alone or not.

But to be on the safe side Szymon had better come down from that loft faster.

The Codger's stopped scanning the station buildings and is walking on. But, look! It's not the station he's heading for. He's turned off into the copse beside Witek's field. Maybe the Codger doesn't know Heddi's come back and is waiting at the station, What do you mean, doesn't know? She's back. He knows that alright; what he doesn't know is that Heddi hasn't come back alone.

There! He's come out of the copse and he's holding an oak stick. Using it for support, he's walking in the direction of the station.

Presumably the Codger knows Heddi hasn't come back alone and is going to use that stick to kill her.

Szymon had better got a move on hitching up the mare, because the Headman's out of breath and slowing his pace, and the Codger's nearing the station.

Go, on he's not that close. It's a good two miles from the hill to the station, so if Szymon hurries, he'll be able to get the Headman there in time.

She was a pretty thing, the Codger's Heddi. She may have grown up even prettier than the Headman's Hedwig once was.

The village boys were mad about her, but the Codger guarded his daughter. He wouldn't let anyone near the girl. For that matter Heddi herself had no time for boys.

Szymon's mare is lame because she cast a shoe yesterday and Szymon was going to see the Blacksmith but he knocked it back at the Witeks' christening and overslept.

The mare is lame and Szymon can't give the Headman a lift.

The Codger must be headed off at all costs. Send the Headman's boy out into the fields and unhitch one of the plough horses. Taking short-cuts he can catch the Codger up in half an hour.

But it's not the Headman's boy who's to head off the Codger, but the Headman himself. And the Headman won't mount a horse, because the last time the Headman got on a horse was at Heddi's christening. That was a good twenty years ago. The Headman knocked it back that time, fell off the horse and damaged his back. Ever since he hasn't been able to ride.

Well, if the Headman can't mount a horse, have Szymon go and head off the Codger.

There's no point in Szymon going because the only person in the village who can stop the Codger is the Headman.

There's nothing for it, but to send the boy to the Commandant. Let the Commandant lend his motorcycle. The Headman won't have any trouble catching up the Codger on a motorcycle.

But the Headman can't ride a motorcycle.

Well then, the Commandant can give the Headman a lift. After all the Commandant ought also to be interested in seeing the Codger doesn't kill Heddi. Because if the Codger kills Heddi it is going to be the Commandant's headache.

In that case the boy had better hurry over to the Commandant, and there's no time to lose because the Codger's less than a mile from the station.

Luckily he seems to have tired, because he's sat down in the ditch and is resting.

What's the Codger doing now?

The Codger's sitting in the ditch and smoking a butt.

There now, the Commandant's come out on his motorcycle, so the Headman will have no trouble catching up the Codger.

The Codger's sitting in the ditch. He's stretched out his legs and unbuttoned his coat. He's smoking a butt and singing.

It's the first time the Codger's sung since Heddi ran away.

Maybe, but the Codger doesn't know that Heddi hasn't come back alone. So that's why he's sitting in the ditch and singing.

The Commandant's caught up with the Headman. The Headman's only halfway up the hill because he knocked it back yesterday at the Witeks' and he's not in the best of shape.

That's torn it! The Headman's announced he won't get on the motorcycle on a bet because he once fell off a horse and has a bad back, and it's very bumpy riding on the pillion.

Well then, let the Commandant head off the Codger by himself. After all if anyone should be interested in seeing the Codger doesn't kill Heddi, it's the Commandant. Because if the Codger does kill Heddi, it's going to be no one but the Commandant's headache.

But there's no point in the Commandant going, because the only person in the village who can stop the Codger is the Headman.

Meanwhile the Codger has got to his feet, brushed off his coat and continued on his way.

The village women were flabbergasted by a man cosseting a child the way the Codger did Heddi. He washed her nappies and fed her out of a bottle. He wouldn't let his old woman near the kid . . .

When she was bigger, Heddi followed him everywhere. The Codger patiently kept pace with her little stride. They frequently stopped for a rest. He sang to her then in a clear, melodious voice.

But yesterday Witek's brother-in-law in the city came to the christening, didn't he? He turned up on a motorcycle with a sidecar, because he had his mother-in-law with him. In the morning he went back alone, so he left the sidecar in the Witeks' yard.

So why doesn't the Commandant go over to the Witeks', collect the sidecar from the yard, put the Headman in the sidecar and get him there in time.

But the gate into the Witeks' yard is locked. Everyone is out in the fields, and by the time Witek can be fetched, the Codger can have reached the station ten times over.

The gate has to be forced. The best thing would be to summon Szymon and have him help the Commandant force the gate. Ah, there's Szymon now.

They seem to be having heavy weather in forcing the gate. No wonder, seeing they were both at the Witeks' christening yesterday. There, and about time too . . .

In ten minutes the Codger will have reached the station. The Headman and the Commandant will have to get a move on, if they're to be in time.

Luckily, the Codger has stopped to attend to a call of nature. In any case he's slackened his pace. He's shuffling along, supported on the stick. He means to kill Heddi with that stick. He must know that Heddi hasn't come back alone.

Szymon's boy, that's learning to be a doctor in the city, fell in love with Heddi. Szymon called on the Codger to ask for the girl's hand.

The Codger was silent a while and then said:

"You've brought your boy up badly, Szymon. He has an itch for other men's wives. He hung around the Headman's Hedwig when her husband was taken off to hospital. I won't give him Heddi!"

The Commandant's motorcycle has bogged down in the sand. They didn't even get as far as the top of the hill.

They won't make it now.

The Codger's just entered the station.

The Priest must be notified. Get him to toll the bell.

A tragedy's brewing.

The Priest hands the organist the key of the bell tower. The organist climbs the steps wheezing because he has been playing all night at the Witeks' christening.

The bell will toll any minute . . .

Heddi arrived in the morning, but now here it is almost evening. She's sitting in the waiting room. She's wrapped her shoulders in a shawl.

The Codger limps up to her. He leans on the stick.

The Codger is silent and Heddi is silent.

"Well, Heddi," the Codger eventually says. "You've come back, Heddi, and you're not alone either!"

Heddi rises from the bench, tears streaming down her face like peas.

The Codger brushes the gray hair from his eyes, steps across to Heddi and takes the bundle from her arms.

"Right," he says, "get your case. Heddi. I've made up the cradle that your dead mother put away in the attic. Come on, Heddi, we're going home!"

The Codger had known all along that Heddi hadn't come back alone.

Maria Nurowska, born in 1944, is a graduate of the University of Warsaw. Her first collection of short stories, Nie strzelaj do organisty, *was published in 1975. She has also published novels and has written for television and radio.*

"It is like swimming in the middle of
a deep river with a crocodile waiting on one bank
and a lion on the other bank."

The Man in the Dust

BY JANE MEIRING

A solemn move has its touch of mirth.

IT was dark and very late when Kalitani made his way back. He went through the bush silently, lightly, afraid of what might be hiding in the bushes. His bare toes felt along the path, avoiding the dry sticks and leaves, as his father had taught him to do long ago when he was a small boy and learning how to track down the *mahara*.

When he reached his village, he heard no voices. Only an owl, a *zizi*, was softly calling from a tree near his father's kraal. And there were no fires.

All about there hung a familiar smell, all too familiar to Kalitani, for he had smelled it often, after the hunt, when the throat of an animal had been cut. And today, when there had been so much blood spilled in his village, that smell was very strong.

The part of his mind which had registered the happenings of the morning was still stunned, and he had difficulty believing that what he had seen and heard was real, that what he had seen writhing on the ground under the sticks had been his father, the headman of the village. Kalitani stood at the edge of the clearing, his heart pounding. Where had they gone?

When the terrorists—the *makandanga*—had taken him away, pushing him roughly ahead of them, they had left in the village the old people who had been forced to watch the killing and the beating. But the young people, the frightened and crying children, had been taken away by the *makandanga* and roughly prodded with the ends of guns when they did not walk fast enough. Only he, Kalitani, sixteen years old and strong, had been clever enough to escape.

Above the soft calling of the *zizi* he heard a new sound coming from his father's kraal. He followed it, stepping over the soft bundles that covered the ground. When he reached it he found his mother.

The District Commissioner held up eight fingers. "In eight days," he said, "in eight days, in the same number of days as you see by my fingers, we will come back and take all of you to a safe place." He waited for Dekudza to interpret. "In eight days," the District Commissioner repeated. "You understand? We will take you to a place where the *makandanga* cannot harm you again."

He looked at the expressionless faces as the interpreter spoke, but there was only a slight stirring in the crowd. The horror of the past days—the attack on the village, the death and destruction and, above all, the taking of their children—was still numbing their minds with grief and fear and shock.

"We are leaving soldiers here to look after and protect you. The young boy, Kalitani, will show us where to find your children and we will bring them back to you if we can. But in eight days' time the trucks will be here to take you far from here, to a village with a high fence and soldiers to look after you. You will have fresh water from the river, and land where you can grow your mealies and your *pfunde* in peace."

In the middle of the crowd a man lifted his hand for permission to speak. Dekudza looked at the District Commissioner, who nodded.

"What if the *makandanga* come back before the eight days are gone?" the man asked. "And what if we are threatened by guns again until we feed them and give them a place to sleep? What then?

Will the Government punish us as others were punished? We are in trouble with the Government and we are in trouble with the *makandanga*. In which direction must we turn? It is like swimming in the middle of a deep river with a crocodile waiting on one bank and a lion on the other bank. What are we to do?" He was an elderly man and his arm hung in a sling dark with dried blood. The people around him nodded and murmured.

"There is nothing to be afraid of," the District Commissioner said. "Dekudza has already told you—we will leave soldiers here to guard you. No one will harm you before we return with the trucks. Those of you who wish to go back to Mozambique may go. Those of you who wish to stay in Rhodesia must be ready when we return. But this place *must* be emptied. Do you understand? Your goats and fowls and your furniture will go with you. But there is no room in the trucks for cattle. All your huts will be burned, as will all your mealie lands, *pfunde* and other crops still growing and not ready for harvesting. You will be given food in your new village. And later on, you will once again be able to grow your own food."

He lifted his hands again, showing them eight fingers. "Eight days."

On the eighth day, when the trucks came, the village people were ready and waiting for them. The huts were smoldering, the plots of land had been dug up and burned. The security forces had found the terrorists' camp and, after a short engagement, had succeeded in rescuing a number of the children and returning them to the village. The people stood together in close family groups with boxes, blankets and pots and a few pieces of furniture.

Major Sanders, in charge of operations, looked round at his men, seasoned members of the R.A.R., who grinned at him, shrugging their shoulders.

He turned to Dekudza. "I did not know there would be so many people."

"They have brought others back from Mozambique," Dekudza explained. "They say it is safer here. They all want to go with us."

"But there aren't enough trucks for all these extra people," Sanders said.

"They do not mind if they are a little squashed," Dekudza said, and went away to hustle up the people.

To make room, some of the villagers' possessions were reluctantly relinquished, and at last the trucks were ready to move out.

The few families whose children were missing seemed unwilling to leave without them. They kept looking wistfully towards the north, although they realized they could wait no longer. The soldiers—the *masojas*—had promised to get them back and now they could only hope that the promise would be kept.

"All right," Sanders called to the driver of the first truck, "get moving and keep a look out all the way. Good luck." He was thinking of ambush and land-mines.

The driver let in the clutch, revved the engine and slowly the truck moved forward, swaying under its load.

"Well, we managed to fit them all in," Sanders said, looking at the other trucks, loaded and ready to move out.

But Dekudza shook his head. "There is one man who wishes to speak with you, sir." He pointed to a crumpled figure sitting in the dirt under a msasa tree. A small, gray donkey stood placidly near by.

"What's wrong with him? Why isn't he on a truck?" Sanders asked.

"He wants to take his donkey," Dekudza explained.

The major exploded. "His donkey!" He jabbed his finger in the direction of the overloaded trucks moving clumsily away one by one. "Donkey!" he shouted incredulously. "A bloody donkey, on top of all that?" He looked at the figure in the dirt. *"Bemhe?* Donkey? You want him to go too?"

The man nodded, smiling.

Sanders pointed to the remaining trucks, loaded beyond capacity. "Can't you see? It's bloody well impossible! There's no room. You'll have to leave the thing here. Come now, hurry up or you'll be left behind." Dekudza interpreted.

The man in the dust lifted his head again. To Dekudza he said, for the major's benefit, "Look—look carefully." Half creeping, half crawling, like an injured spider, he dragged his shriveled legs after him through the dust until he reached the donkey. He climbed up the front legs of the animal with an unexpected grace and agility. Now seated on the back of the donkey he was suddenly transformed into a human being.

He looked across at the major and laughed. His laughter was happy and full of pride. "See!" he said. "Now I am a man! A chief! A lion! And with my four strong legs I can move! I can go anywhere!" He pointed to the ground. "Down there I am nothing, for there on the ground I am like a beetle that a child has crushed with his small foot. Up here I am a man and I am alive!"

Major Sanders bit his lip. He understood the man's dilemma but he had problems of his own. He looked at his men. They shrugged their shoulders; the responsibility lay with their commanding officer. He knew it and they knew it. In despair he looked at the two remaining trucks. The others could be heard toiling down the road into the valley. There was absolutely no space—perhaps for one more man, but for a donkey . . .!

He wanted to laugh but the sight of the man sitting on his donkey in all his smiling pride, confident that all he had to do was ask and it would be done, filled him with frustration and anger.

"No, no!" he shouted. "I cannot take the donkey. It's impossible! Where do I put it? Don't you see, you bloody old idiot, that there's no room?"

For a few seconds the man stared in disbelief. Then he slid down the front legs of the donkey and once more dissolved into a bundle of rags in the dirt. "Yes, yes, I understand," he said quietly. "It is right, there is no room; there is no space for an animal. We cannot ask for everything."

Dekudza reminded him that it was time to get on to the truck and go.

"Go?" the man said in astonishment. "Like this? Like a crushed beetle? Without my donkey? Without my strong four legs?"

Dekudza nodded, as impatient as the others to be gone.

The man calmly looked up at him. "You must shoot me before you go, for like this I cannot go with you. I do not care. It does not worry me to die. I have seen much death in this village, of people who were strong and useful. When an animal is old and useless it is killed. Therefore that time has come for me too."

He looked across at Major Sanders. "You do it," he beseeched him, "for you have a strong gun."

When Dekudza had translated the man's words, Sanders walked over to his vehicle. The soldiers, and the tribesmen in all their simplicity and faith, waited to see what he would do. The moment of decision, the decision itself, suddenly assumed tremendous significance. He picked up his walkie-talkie and called his base. "Oscar Base, Oscar Base, this is Charlie Mobile, do you read me? Over."

A few seconds later a voice crackled back at him. "Charlie Mobile, read you strength five. Over."

"Can you send me a helicopter? Over."

"A helicopter? What the devil for? Have you wounded? Over."

"No. All wounded are on trucks on their way out. Over."

"Why a helicopter? Over."

"To move a bloody donkey out. Over."

The crackle that came back to him was not all atmospherics. "A donkey? Dammit all, Charlie Mobile, have you gone crazy or something? Over."

"Yes, I do think I'm crazy but I need the 'copter. It's absolutely essential. Over."

"Essential? Over."

"Yes. Say for morale, if you like. Look, Oscar Base, you know me well enough. I wouldn't ask for it unless I believed it was absolutely essential. Over."

"O.K. O.K. Wilco."

Sanders had the last two trucks wait behind for the helicopter. The people, apprehensive and suspicious, got out slowly. When Dekudza spoke to them, trying to explain, some of them glared resentfully at the man and his donkey.

Two hours later the helicopter appeared, stuttering and roaring over their heads, the long rotors flashing round—an awesome spectacle for the tribespeople. It hovered over the trees and, like a great dragonfly, gently came down in the clearing.

The villagers climbed quickly into the trucks and watched open-mouthed as Dekudza and the donkey's owner were bundled into the seats behind the pilot. They broke out into an excited babble when a wide girth-strap was tied round the donkey's body, and then burst into laughter, their troubles momentarily forgotten, when the helicopter slowly lifted itself off the ground and moved off with the kicking animal dangling below it.

It was Dekudza's first ride in a helicopter and he was tremendously excited. But the old man beside him was paralyzed with fear. However, as the machine climbed higher and higher, and turned south, he gradually relaxed. Soon he was looking down through the bubble-glass on to the world so far below. And after a while he looked at Dekudza and began to chuckle.

It was a solemn occasion for Dekudza and he was shocked. "What is the matter?" he asked. "Why do you laugh?"

The man grinned at him. "You must tell the big *masoja* that if we reach that village of safety without any further trouble I shall no longer be satisfied with the four legs of my little donkey. They are far too slow for me. From now on this is the way I would like to travel. Like this! Like a bird! No longer like a tick on the back of a beast!"

Born in 1920 in South Africa, Jane Meiring is a journalist, short story and radio script writer and author of five books. She lived for some time in Zimbabwe (formerly Rhodesia) and has now returned to South Africa.

"He hissed a warning note to the goose swimming by his side."

Spring Will Come

BY FRED D. BERKEBILE

The faithfulness of wildlife.

THE weird sound of coarse honking cries, high in the dark morning sky, announced the arrival of the gray geese. Calling at regular intervals, they dropped down through the darkness and circled slowly over the lake in the center of a large swamp. Leveling off sharply above the choppy surface, they struck the water with two distinct splashing sounds.

There were but two geese in the flight—a gander and a goose. They swam about rapidly for a few minutes on the rough water, then paused to fluff and reset their feathers. With the first streaks of dawn, both swam directly toward a grass and bulb covered shoreline of the windswept lake.

The gander was uneasy and suspicious as he swam shoreward in the gray dawn. Experience warned him that the morning dawn—a favorite time for wild geese to feed—was also the most opportune period for his enemies to lay in wait for him. He listened attentively for strange sounds above the noise of whistling wind and lapping waves splashing against his rump and wings. Satisfied that no immediate danger lay in the offing, he spread his wings outward and stretched upward to his full three and one-half foot height. He shook the spray from his grayish black feathers and thrust his black beak into the water. Then slowly moving shoreward, he watched the line of cattails and reeds for signs of possible enemies.

During a prolonged lull between gusts of wind, he noted a slight unnatural movement among the tallest cattails. He hissed a warning note to the goose swimming by his side. He quickly swam off at a right angle and spread his wings to flee, but his mate ignored his warning cry and continued to swim shoreward. He hissed again, kicked his powerful webbed feet deep in the water, and moved rapidly away, against the raw wind and the slapping white capped waves. The gander hesitated. Hunger after the long tiresome flight assailed him. The shoreline promised food. He swung about and slowly rejoined his mate. The gander had learned, in the past few years to excercise the utmost caution when approaching land or food. He and the goose had mated three years before, and their first brood of goslings had fallen into the clutches of an eagle. The second year they had selected a nesting place on a marshy mound near the lake; but before the young could fly, a red fox had scented their hiding place, and one by one the vixen had carried the goslings into the nearby forest.

The past year the two geese found a well-protected area close by the lake but despite their utmost caution, most of their brood of half-grown goslings again fell victim to the sharp-eyed eagle and the ever-hunting red fox. And finally, a thin-faced, sharp-featured poacher happened upon the last two goslings and carried them off to his car. So, now, the suspicious and experienced gander thrust his head to one side and minutely examined every stalk, bush, stump, or fallen tree before he continued toward the shore.

Directly facing the advancing geese, the same thin-faced poacher sat waiting in a cunningly devised blind hidden among the clump of cattails. Watching the approaching geese intently, his crafty, steel-gray eyes glinted with anticipation. The man shifted his legs without moving his arms. His soiled, long fingers closed firmly about the stock and forearm of his well worn shotgun. He moved slightly to gain a better shooting position. His slow, measured movements were almost imperceptible as he shifted the muzzle of his gun toward the incoming geese.

The hunter's face twisted into an expression of grim satisfaction, for he had predicted that the geese would return this spring to their old nesting area, despite the fact that they had lost their brood the past summer. The man's muscles tensed still more at the steady approach of the hungry and travel-weary birds. Cautiously he shifted the gun forward, determined that these last two geese should also be his. He experienced a keen delight and inward satisfaction in wantonly killing wild creatures. During late October he had killed the last remaining woodchuck in the area as it sat at the mouth of its solitary burrow for a last glimpse of the warm sunshine, before hibernating. Also, on the last day of the legal hunting season, he had grinned with exultation as the only grouse in the swamp fell amid a burst of feathers before his shotgun. A ringneck pheasant cock had eluded his marksmanship during open season, but fell victim to one of his snares baited with corn grains. The two wild geese were creatures that had yearly escaped the man's gun, the snare, and his greed. The poacher's small gray eyes narrowed. The unsuspecting geese were swimming steadily forward and were almost within range of his heavily loaded shotgun.

As they neared the shore, the two geese veered sharply to the hunter's right and swam toward a section of the shoreline where bulbs and luscious swamp grass grew in profusion. They fed hurriedly in the shallow water and as they ate moved slowly toward the cattails that hid the hunter. The gander still suspicious of the unnatural formation of cattails forming the blind, reared high to study the formation. The belated sun broke through a narrow rift in the heavy clouds and threw long shafts of golden light through the foggy atmosphere. Wary and alert, the gander noted a glint of sunlight reflecting from the smooth gun barrel, it lit up the hunter's brown cap and oval face. The gander flared out his broad wings, thrust his head higher, and screamed a warning to his feeding mate.

With outstretched necks, the two geese splashed away through the weeds and shallow water. Beating their powerful wings on the choppy waves, they moved slowly away from the reeds and cattails. Slowly they left the surface of the water and flew toward the center of the lake.

Still honking a loud warning, the gander beat his wings frantically as the poacher reared upright from the cattails. The man threw the gun to his shoulder and fired. The gander dropped downward and then upward as the shotgun pellets ripped through his heavy feathers and seared the flesh on his back. He screamed with pain and fear and swerved off to the left when the gun cracked again. His mate was lying with wings outspread on the surface of the lake. A puff of feathers whirled above her.

The poacher fired two more blasts. The pellets rattled harmlessly against the gander's wings as he climbed higher. Then courageously, he circled back slowly to fly lower over his struggling and wounded mate.

The goose called a shrill warning. With one wing dragging she swam quickly away from the dangerous shoreline.

Despite her warning cries, the gander circled lower and splashed down by her side. Then he and the wounded goose swam desperately against the strong wind and pounding waves. The poacher's gun roared again, but now both geese were well beyond the range of the vicious pellets. As the geese headed for the center of the lake, the gander poked curiously at his mate's broken wing then uttered low cries as if to encourage her to swim faster. They finally came to rest on the opposite shore. There the goose plucked away the soiled wing feathers and tried futiley to draw the broken wing to her side. The gander swam about his mate in close circles and honked loud challenges to the crafty-eyed poacher, who at that moment was being driven from the cattails by the angry owner of the lake and surrounding swamp.

Later in the year the painful wing prevented the goose from mating. However, both geese stayed close together while searching for food along the shoreline and retreated to the center of the lake after feeding. They sat there in morose and sullen quietude throughout the day.

Summer and early autumn passed quickly. The wind brought down the brightly colored leaves and roared among the bare limbs.

The first freezing weather sent flocks of noisy wild ducks winging southward. But the two geese stayed on the lake. Snow now swirled in from the north and drifted in huge banks over the reeds and cattails. Mud-specked ice formed along the shoreline and spread outward. Finally the ice-pack froze about them until only a small circular space of open water remained. This they managed to keep open by swimming about in circles and pecking away the ice that threatened to imprison them.

The storm passed but the clear weather brought more freezing temperature down over the swamp. During the intensely cold nights, the water froze more closely about the two stranded geese until only a tiny opening remained. Both geese pecked constantly at the ever closing circle and kept treading the water with broad webbed feet to keep the space open. Finally, the coldest part of the winter moved in. The geese deprived of food had grown weak and faced not only death from freezing, but starvation as well. The gander honked loudly at intervals. He spread his wings frequently to suggest he was impatient to be off for the southland, but he steadfastly refused to leave his wounded mate.

One cold clear evening, the farmer who owned the swamp and lake noticed the two geese stranded in the center of the sheet of ice. Cautiously, he skated out toward them. The gander filled with dread of men and guns saw him approaching. He climbed from the open water and stood on the ice, undecided whether to stay by his mate and fight off the two-legged skater, or take flight. The man was almost upon him before the gander cried out loudly, fluttered his broad wings, skidded awkwardly about and slowly took flight.

The gander circled overhead and honked in protest as the farmer caught the fluttering goose. Her weird, pitiful cries echoed over the dismal, wind-swept lake and swamp. The man held the struggling goose close to his breast and skated back to the shore and carried the goose to his barn.

The gander flew in low over the barnyard, calling encouragement to his mate. He continued to circle about until the man entered the barn and closed the great wooden door. In the gathering dusk of early evening he continued to fly over the barn calling at regular intervals. He heard the muffled sound of cackling hens and the noisy cries of domesticated ducks, and as they died down, he made one more flight over the barn. He called loudly and caught the goose's weak response. Then as if despairing of helping his wounded mate, he swung about in the raw winter wind. With a kind of grim determination he flew higher into the darkening sky and headed southward.

From a dust-covered window in the barn the farmer watched the gander until he disappeared in the distance. Later in the evening, the man came back into the barn and with the help of his wife, forced the goose to eat a warm gruel of bran and sweet milk. Carefully the farmer placed the goose in a slatted, straw-filled packing box and left her for the night.

In a short time the goose grew fat and sleek. Her feathers glinted in the bright sunlight as she wandered about inside the closely woven wirefence surrounding the barnyard. Her broken wing had healed, but was useless for flight or for striking down disturbing chickens or domesticated geese, the noisy ducks, or the man's dog. She quickly accepted the man and his wife as a part of her daily life, and grew quite gentle and tame.

Heavy warm rains and gusting south winds, the usual harbingers of spring brought insistent and constant advances from unattached, domesticated ganders, but the crippled wild goose evaded or ignored their attention. Quietly she continued to keep away from the ganders. She had lost her mate, and by nature refused to become interested. She grew sullen and morose as the warm spring rains melted the last of the deep snow from the nearby hillside and the other fowls spent more of the daylight hours in the muddy barnyard. Each day she ate the food placed before her, and then retired to sulk in a far corner of the yard.

During the lengthening days the goose would occasionally turn her black head to one side to scrutinize the scudding, low spring clouds. At other times she would suddenly snap her head from under her wing and listen attentively. Once when a flock of wild ducks flew low over the barnyard headed for their northern nesting ground, she grew nervous and excited. She ran from her isolated corner and standing well out near the center of the barnyard, honked wildly and cackled shrilly to the swiftly flying birds. After the passage of the ducks, she retired to her corner and again sat in sullen silence.

Most of the domesticated geese had mated. Some of the geese had nests half-filled with ivory tinted eggs; others had filled their nests and grown broody, sitting out the long, tiresome four weeks until the clutches of eggs were hatched. The injured goose kept well away from the brooding geese and either walked slowly about the barnyard, or stood moodily in her favorite corner, where she kept her eyes on the speckled spring skies.

Early one brisk, gray spring morning, when the low flying clouds scudded above the muddy barnyard, every chicken, duck, and goose was set to cackling, calling, or honking. Far off in the south, high in the sky, a peculiar, hoarse honking had electrified all the barnyard fowl. And well above the wild clamor of the other birds the wild goose raised her own shrill voice. The familiar, encouraging sound came closer and finally passed swiftly overhead. The chickens, ducks, and domesticated geese regained their composure and went back to their feeding, but the wild goose stayed in the center of the yard, sending out her plaintive shrill cries long after the last raucous honking had died in the distance. Finally she returned to her corner and sat silent and motionless throughout the long day.

The following morning, long before dawn, the young farmer entered the barn to attend to his morning chores. He held a lantern aloft and looked over the poultry. Outside the wind howled in the face of a northeast storm. A heavy rain beat noisily against the dusty barn windows. He started toward the cow stall. Suddenly a familiar hoarse cry sounded faintly above the roaring wind and pounding rain. He paused to listen to the honking sound and the crippled goose's sudden noisy movements. He studied the captive wild goose curiously as she fluttered her one wing and screamed shrilly. She cried out again and again and finally ran to the closed shed door and started to cackle furiously.

The youthful farmer put down the lantern, stepped briskly to the shed door, and pushed it wide open. He stood out in the wind and rain and watched the fluttering goose run out in the gray dawn, to send her anxious cackling cries into the roaring storm.

But the solitary honking cry far above the heavy storm clouds faded in the distance, and the wild goose lowered her head in silence. Then she reared her black head high and appeared to be listening attentively. There were no sounds other than the noise of the wind and rain. The farmer went back into the barn, caught up the lantern and came back to the shed door. He lowered the lantern and swung, it to and fro nervously, as he watched the goose lower her head, curve it back over her feathers. The goose shook her short tail and flicked raindrops right and left. She looked appealingly at the farmer, who left the wide barn door open.

The northeast wind whined dismally between the slats of the half-empty corncrib. Heavy raindrops splashed on the huge puddles of dull, muddy water. Grayish black clouds scudded low over the barn, the man, and the goose.

Suddenly, almost directly above the muddy barnyard, resounded the sharp, clear honking of the gander. Above the noise of the wind and the rain, he had heard the muffled cries of his mate and had circled back from his northern flight.

The goose thrust her head skyward, cackled wildly, and fluttered her broken and useless wing.

The young farmer placed his lantern in the mud, scooped up the fluttering goose, and carried her over to the steel gate. He pushed open the latch and swung the gate wide. As gently as he might handle a young child, the farmer put the goose down on the pathway leading down to the swamp and the lake. He smiled indulgently as the goose whipped about and hissed before she ran forward, neck outstretched, toward the rising sun and the open lake. The farmer smiled, closed the steel gate and watched the honking gander sweeping downward under the heavy, dark clouds, to splash noisily down upon the choppy lake. A place where he would spend the spring and coming summer with his crippled mate.

Autumn came and went without a mishap to the geese and their brood of goslings. Winter again crept down from the northland, but the family of geese remained on the lake until the shallow water along the shoreline started to freeze. One frigid morning a new storm threatened from the north and west. High winds and colder weather was in the offing. About high noon, the old gander left the lake, followed by the eleven young geese. Anxiously, he swung about the broad lake, followed by the noisy young geese flying instinctively in perfect "V" formation. The geese honked and called constantly to the crippled goose. She answered the plaintive cries several times and then fell silent.

The old gander and the young geese circled the lake several times, gaining altitude with each flight. As the darkening clouds banked higher in the north and the raw wind ruffled the water, the long formation flew directly southward.

The last faint honking sounds died away in the rising wind. The lone goose sat quietly on the choppy water, head cocked, and watched intently until the formation disappeared beyond the gray black clouds. She dipped her short crooked beak into the freezing water, shook her short black tail feathers, and without a backward glance, swam directly toward the little pathway leading from the lake to the comfortable warm barn.

That night the goose was back in the barn with the chickens and the domesticated geese. She found her favorite corner, with its fresh straw and wheat chaff. She settled down for the night, waiting for another bitter winter to pass and for the warm spring winds to bring to her anxious ears the honking cries of her faithful mate and the young geese. She thrust her head under her broken wing, confident that spring would come.

Fred D. Berkebile made time for his writing. He served in the Pennsylvania public schools as teacher, principal and supervisor. He also taught at several colleges. During World War II Major Berkebile served in Africa and Europe with many units. He was Chairman of the Education Department of the Army University. Major Berkebile wrote under his own name and several pseudonyms, publishing over 200 short stories, articles and newspaper columns in addition to several novels. He enjoyed working with themes highlighting the beauties of nature.

"The birds know when something big
is coming, and get out of the way."

Richter 10

BY L.A.P. MOORE

**Events in the realm of fiction . . .
fiction at this time.**

IT was a cold, cloudless night at the Nuclear Test Site in the Nevada desert, 50 miles northeast of Death Valley. The moon had already set behind the mountains, and the stars glittered like ice crystals in the black sky. The brilliant flashes of blue, red, white, and green from Sirius, the Dog Star, went unnoticed as the final seconds ticked away. At exactly 4 a.m., the ground shuddered from the shock of the most powerful nuclear bomb ever exploded beneath the surface of the earth.

The first murmur of the San Andreas Fault was not recorded until almost an hour later. It was a gentle murmur, registering 2.4 on the Richter Scale, and centered about 20 miles southeast of Palmdale, in Southern California.

"Did you hear that?" asked Mary as she turned off the 8 a.m. news. Shanty Irish, and proud of it, Mary had long, deep-red hair and pale blue eyes that seemed to reflect rather than absorb.

Shawn wandered out of the bathroom drying his heavily muscled back. He was a large, strong, gentle man. "Did I hear what?"

"There was an earthquake down south. Every time I hear about one near the San Andreas I start thinking. We're only six miles from Bodega Bay, and it's right on top of the fault. What would happen if an earthquake hit here right now?"

"Kiss me quick! It may be our last chance!"

"I'm going to do more than that to you, if you don't go put some clothes on." Starting at the corners of his mouth, and spreading from ear to ear, a large grin grew on Shawn's face. Mary watched it grow, dropped her eyes about a yard, and turned off the kitchen stove.

The 30-foot antenna at JPL in Pasadena, California is one of the eyes of ARIES (Astronomical Radio Interferometric Earth Survey-ing). The other is the 210-foot antenna at NASA's Deep Space Network in Goldstone, 125 miles to the east, and on the other side of the San Andreas Fault. Both are watching the same 20 quasars, as far as a billion light-years from earth. Using this system, the ARIES staff have determined the distance between the two antennae to within four inches. At 8:27 a.m., that distance increased by a few millimeters—too small a change for even this inter-galactic system to notice.

Mary, Hank, Moon, and Shawn had come into the mail house from their cabins, and were grouped around the warmth of the kitchen stove when Sam and Adam entered.

"Good morning," Sam said as he and Adam followed their noses across the room to the coffee pot. Sam, a long, lanky, easy-going person, talked a lot and laughed easily—almost the opposite of Adam.

"Did you hear about the earthquake?" Mary asked.

"Yeah," answered Sam. "Just caught the tail end of it, but it was somewhere near the Mexican border . . . El Centro, that was it."

"The one I heard about on the 8 o'clock news was near Palmdale."

"Couldn't have been the same one, then. The one near El Centro happened about 8:30."

"Got some surfboards?" chimed in Hank. "We could make it clear to Salt Lake City on the wave The Big One's going to make." He was very proud of his body, and had taken up surfing mainly to show it off. Hank seldom just stood—he posed.

Loner wandered into the kitchen wearing her "not quite awake" smile.

"Here's our earthquake expert now," said Hank, handing her a cup of coffee.

Loner believed that clothes should be sturdy rather than decorative, and dressed that way; her voice often took on a tone that varied from tired to distracted.

"You've read a lot about geology, haven't you Loner?" Shawn asked.

"Mmmm," answered Loner through the steam rising from her mug.

"There was a quake near Palmdale before 8 this morning, and then another one near El Centro about 8:30. Think we're going to get The Big One?" Sam asked.

"No way to tell. There are thousands of quakes in California every year, but not many big enough to feel. Charles Richter says the San Andreas moves in three sections—south, central, and north—and they're all due for a big one."

"What about the Richter Scale?" asked Mary. "Is a Richter 8 twice as big as a Richter 4? And what do those numbers really mean, anyway?"

"The Richter Scale is easy once you know the secret. Each whole number up means sixty times as much energy is released. A Richter 2 earthquake releases sixty times as much energy as a Richter 1, and a Richter 3 releases sixty times as much as a Richter 2. What the numbers really mean is simple, too. A Richter 1 can't be felt by people, only by instruments. A Richter 2 can just barely be felt if you're standing right on top of it. A Richter 4.5 can be felt for about 20 miles, and can cause slight damage. A Richter 6+ can be fairly destructive, and will do a lot of damage in built-up areas. A Richter 7+ is called a Major Earthquake, and a Richter 8+ is called a Great Earthquake. There have been only three Great Earthquakes in

California since people started writing them down a couple of hundred years ago: 1857 in Tejon Pass in Southern California; 1872 in Owens Valley in eastern Central California; and 1906 near Olema in Northern California. The one centered near Olema is the one people call The Great San Francisco Earthquake; it was an 8.3."

"You've stirred me into action," Shawn said in his slow, deep voice. "I'm going to look the place over to see if there's anything that needs doing."

"Not as good as surfboards," Sam decided, "but not an all-bad idea. I'll go with you."

"I'll be in the garage working on the truck, and then up fixing the pump," Adam said. "Come get me if you need a hand."

The family had four major celebration days: Winter Solstice ("sol stops") when the sun reaches its southernmost point in the sky, about December 22nd; Spring Equinox ("equal night") when night and day are equal and the sun crosses the equator heading north, about March 21st; Summer Solstice, when the sun reaches its northernmost point, about June 21st; and Autumn Equinox, when the sun crosses the equator heading south, about September 23rd. Today was the day of the Spring (or Vernal) Equinox, and a feast was planned for early afternoon. In the meantime, it was a normal day at the farm.

Hank and Mary were working on one of the four cabins the family used as their private rooms. Hank looked up to the west and said, "Looks like every bird along the coast is coming inland."

"Might be a storm heading in. The birds know when something big is coming, and get out of the way. That combination bomb/storm/wine cellar we dug into the hill may come in handy yet. As Shawn says, 'If you've got to hole-up somewhere, it'd be hard to beat a wine cellar.' "

"I'll stick to dope. Too much booze'd ruin my perfect body," said Hank, posing like Mr. Universe.

"Good—then it'd match your ruin of a mind. Hand me another 4X4, and we're just about done with this bed loft. Those guys are crazy wanting a waterbed 8 feet off the floor. That much water weighs about a ton, not to mention the rice paddy they'd have for a floor if it sprung a leak."

At 10 a.m. the U.S. Geological Survey's National Center for Earthquake Research, located just south of San Francisco at Menlo Park, recorded a moderate earthquake in an uninhabited area of the desert about 100 miles from Needles. Since there was no one killed or spectacularly maimed, the people who decide what's news would have ignored it if there hadn't been other earthquake items earlier that day. As it was, they devoted a single sentence to it, followed by a sentence saying that Mauna Loa on the island of Hawaii was erupting again, as it does about every three years. Another single sentence told of a possible underground nuclear weapon test, or earthquake, not far inland from China's coast.

Moon finished the embroidery on Shawn's shirt, put it with the rest of the family's clothes which she had repaired or decorated, and went into the kitchen. Preparation of the Vernal Equinox feast was in the collective hands of Loner, Sam, and Moon. A huge tom turkey had been roasting since the wee hours of the morning. Moon, being a vegetarian, was handling the vegetables; Sam had made the stuffing, including one tablespoon per serving of the powdery dope Hank had left in the blender too long; Loner was washing bowls and pots and pans as fast as they were available. By 1 p.m., when Loner went out on the kitchen porch to ring the "almost ready" warning on the dinner bell, another warning bell was ringing at Menlo Park.

A 4.5 quake had been recorded about 10 miles off the coast southwest of Eureka. This wasn't unusual, as the underwater shelf in this area was known to be a seismically-active area, and shocks were recorded here several times a year. What set the bell off was the almost-simultaneous occurrence of a small quake in the Hoadley-Melones fault area running across the north end of California's vast Central Valley. The Melones fault zone runs close to Folsom and Oroville dams on the southeast, and the Hoadley close to Trinity and Shasta dams on the northwest. Although it was a minor shock, warnings went out for all of the major dams in the area to be inspected closely, and for the flood-gate controls to be manned. If seismic activity picked up in the area, the lakes would be lowered as fast as possible without flooding the areas down-river. This was a routine, but not very practical procedure. It would take weeks to lower the lake levels significantly without causing flooding. With the past winter's rains, and the current run-off from the snow melting in the mountains, the lakes were at their maximum capacity, and the rivers below them were at their annual high-water marks.

The bell sounded a second time, and Adam, Shawn, Hank, and Mary appeared as if through the walls. The family sat down and joined hands around the table in communion, and quiet and peace settled down around them. Everybody started with what was in front of him, and passed it to his left. Then Sam, beaming a Santa Claus smile, walked around the table giving everyone a generous portion of his magic stuffing. Everything on the table was home-grown, including the turkey, and therefore tasted twice as good. Not surprisingly, the conversation had returned to earthquakes.

"There are three big deals," Loner was saying, "plates, rifts, and trenches. The earth is a ball of molten rock and metal. There's a crust of cooled material on the surface, like the film you get on top of a pan of boiled milk when it's cooling. The earth's not flat like the top of the milk, though, so the crust is broken into pieces, and these pieces are the ten plates. Underneath the oceans are huge mountain chains which are split lengthwise down the middle. These rifts in the mountain chains go right down through the earth's crust into the molten mantle beneath. New material oozes up through these rifts constantly, pushing the plates on either side away. The planet is only so big around, though, and that's where the trenches come in. The trenches are places where two plates are bumping head-on, and one is going underneath the other. As the old plate sinks back down into the mantle, it melts. And that, basically, is the cycle."

"What makes quakes along the San Andreas?" Mary asked.

"The plates are all different shapes, and moving all different directions. They don't always bump head-on and make a trench. The San Andreas Fault is where the Pacific Plate is moving northwest and rubbing against the North American Plate. In about 10 million years Los Angeles, which is on the Pacific Plate, will be up next to San Francisco, which is just barely on the North American Plate. When the plates hang-up on each other, and can't slide by, pressure builds up in the rocks along the fault until the pressure is so great that it fractures the rocks where it's hung-up, and jerks on past. That's an earthquake."

The strain gauges built into the semicircle of major dams around the north end of the Central Valley climbed slowly, but there were no new shocks. The dam crews were checking every square centimeter of the dams, looking for any crack, any seeping water, any visible sign of trouble. If the strain gauges were still climbing at 2 p.m., they would begin to release water. They would be warned by the people at Menlo Park if there were any new seismic activity in their area.

"The people in Los Angeles and the people in San Francisco think that they live on the same piece of the earth," Loner continued, "but they don't. California doesn't exist. It was created by politicians, by drawing lines on a map. Earth never heard of California. Los Angeles and San Francisco are on different sides of a very real rift in the earth's crust, the San Andreas Fault. In the 1906 quake, 270 miles of the San Andreas moved. We're like fleas studying the movements of a sleeping dog. Just wait until that dog wakes up."

Goldstone and Pasadena crept another few millimeters apart, quietly and with no fuss.

The floor of the main house rose gently, and then lowered gently, as if the house were floating on the ocean and a wave had just rolled under it. No one spoke except the old house, which groaned and creaked and settled, like some ancient man who had been disturbed in his sleep but not awakened.
    "What was that?" Sam asked. "Did the foundation shift?"
    "I don't think so," Shawn said. "That would have been a sharper feel, and there should be a tilt to the floor. Let's go out and take a look."
    Everybody went out to look at the foundation, leaving the remains

of a truly memorable feast behind them. Outside, nothing seemed different.

"That was strange . . .," said Moon—and was startled by the loudness of her own voice. Everything was quiet. There were no bird or insect sounds, and none of the family animals was making a sound—not even the constantly-fussing chickens. As if questioning the silence, one of the dogs barked, and sound flowed back into the world.

"What's going on around here?" asked Sam. "Let's turn on the radio and see if it's just us."

". . . belly-button deodorant will help you get ahead in your business life, and increase your sex-appeal. Remember—Adam & Eve Belly-Button Deodorant. And now back to our continuing coverage of the rash of earth movements which have occurred since early this morning. The first was near Palmdale, about 5 a.m. Then, about 8:30, there was another near El Centro. Since then, there have been reports of minor earthquakes near Needles, Eureka, and in the north end of the Central Valley. We have checked with the State Water Authority, and have been assured that the four major dams in the area of this latest tremor were not affected, and would not be even in the unlikely event of a major earthquake. On the same topic but further from home, small earth tremors and minor volcanic activity have been reported all around the Pacific. If anything new develops, we'll let you know. Stay tuned to this, your instant-news station."

"Was that an earthquake?" asked Moon. "It felt more like a wave."

"It probably was," answered Loner. "That's one type of earth movement you can get from an earthquake."

"Hey Shawn, what did you and Sam find on your earthquake inspection tour?" Hank asked.

"We were looking for a place where nothing could fall on us, where we couldn't fall off of anything, and where broken electric lines couldn't reach us. The garden seems like the best place. If you feel anything like an earthquake, run for the garden, and don't stop for anything."

"Since there seems to be a whole lot of shaking going on," Sam

added, "it might be a good idea to take everything heavy or break-
able down and put it on the floor for awhile. And if it does happen,
how about turning off the main electric breaker, the propane tank,
and the main water line at the redwood tank?"

"You don't want to mess around near those things during a
quake," Shawn said, "but as soon as it's over, that's a good idea.
There might be more shocks coming, or the lines might be broken."

"Hey" said Sam. "How's about sleeping out tonight. It's Vernal
Equinox, and there's going to be a full moon."

At 2 p.m. the strain gauges on the dams were still creeping up, and
approval for releasing water had come from the Water Authority.
Politicians and police down the lengths of the Sacramento, Feather,
and American rivers had been notified, but the water was going to be
released so slowly that it shouldn't cause any flooding. Nothing was
to be said to the public, "so as to avoid any unnecessary concern."
The water-flow schedule was coordinated with the ocean tides at the
Golden Gate so there wouldn't be any backing-up of the water
between there and the area where the Feather River and the American River joined the Sacramento. The Shasta-Trinity reservoir complex holds close to 10 million acre-feet of water: about 435 billion
cubic feet, or 3 trillion gallons. The Oroville-Folsom complex holds
another 5 million acre-feet.

While Mary and Sam went to make the animal buildings as
earthquake-proof as possible, Hank, Moon, and Loner took the
inside of the house, and Shawn and Adam went off to check the
utility shut-offs and the garage. Nobody really believed they were
going to be hit by a major earthquake, but everybody was afraid (and
a little hopeful) that they might. Everything was in shape by 4 p.m.,
and the family were sitting around the living room waiting for the
news. After the usual news about the rich and powerful of the world,
there was a recap of the day's seismic activity, now including a 5.3
quake south of Point Arena about 2:30.

"That's must be the one we felt," Mary said. "Point Arena's only
60 miles north of here. Isn't it there that the San Andreas is supposed
to go back underwater?"

"Right, six miles north of the Point, at Alder Creek," volunteered

Loner.

"Do you think the San Andreas is going to let go?" Moon asked no one in particular.

"Don't sound so hopeful," Hank jibed, trying to relax the tension he heard in Moon's voice. "These little quakes take some of the strain off, so there's less chance of a big one."

There was a nervous pause, and then Adam said, "Sam's idea of sleeping out sounds better and better."

Not far south of Death Valley, and about 35 miles northeast of Barstow on a dead-end road, is one of the most secret places in the world: Fort Irwin. Here, several Very Important Persons from the worlds of politics, military, and science were convincing one another of the impossibility of their early-morning nuclear bomb explosion having anything to do with the series of earthquakes being reported.

About 350 miles west-northwest of Fort Irwin, on the other side of the San Andreas Fault, the scientists at Menlo Park were finding a pattern in the earth's shiftings, and were convinced that the nuclear bomb was a part of that pattern—was, in fact, the trigger which had set off not only a nuclear chain reaction, but a geological one as well. They were trying to decide whether or not to recommend to the Governor that he issue a public earthquake warning, or even put the state's Earthquake Emergency Plan into effect. If they did, and there were no natural disaster, they would have a man-made one on their hands. The Plan called for the evacuation of all heavily populated areas near known fault zones, including the Los Angeles Basin and the San Francisco Bay Area.

Shawn and Sam were down by the pond, lazing in the warm, late-afternoon sun. Shawn was thinking vaguely about the bottle of Bushmill's Irish Whiskey which Mary had given him for St. Patrick's Day. Sam rolled over on his back to let the sun warm his other side, and said, "Loner seems so sad."

"More than Adam?"

"Oh, Adam's not really sad. He's just deep and quiet, and sometimes it looks like sad."

Shawn thought for a moment, then said, "I don't think Loner's really sad either. She knows more than she understands, and it scares her a little, that's all."

"Why doesn't she pair-up with somebody?"

"Pairing-up is the most common way for people, but not the only way, and not the best one for everybody. Sometimes people live completely alone, and sometimes they live with more than one other person. She's not alone, because she belongs to a family. You just mean that she's not sleeping with anybody regularly. Most people sleep alone most of the time, even if there's somebody else there."

Sam nodded, and changed the subject. "Guess I'd better get the animals looked after."

Shawn smiled, and said he'd see him back at the house.

Each small earthquake, starting with the one from the bomb, relaxed a small part of the complex California fault system. Each time the tension was relaxed at one of these places where a fault was held together, the tension on the system as a whole increased. This was normal, but the extent of the minor quakes was not. The chain reaction was increasing, when theory said it should have been damping down. Would it stop, or would it get worse? The people at Menlo Park decided to wait until 6 o'clock, gathering all the data they could in the meantime, before making a decision.

Hank came in just as the sun was going down, and announced that he had the potbelly stove going in the bathhouse by the pond, and that it would be ready for a sauna by the time they got there. Everyone except Adam, who said he'd be down soon, headed off for the bathhouse. The full moon was just clearing Sonoma Mountain to the east as they passed the garden. It was huge, and a dark red/orange.

"My grandmother used to call that 'Blood on the Moon,' and said it meant that someone was going to die," Mary said.

"That's a safe prophecy—somebody's always dying," retorted Hank.

"Somebody's always being born, too," Moon got in just before Loner ended the conversation with, "If you two don't knock off that morbid stuff, you're going to be who's going to die."

137

Adam sat staring across the meadow, watching dusk climb the redwoods as the sun set. With his dark hair, dark complexion, and very dark eyes, he seemed more part of the black of night than of the light of day, and he was. As the lower trunks turned from brown to silhouette-black, the upper parts were bathed with a rich, golden light. The birds were scurrying through the air in all directions, trying to find just the right place from which to watch the sunset. Within minutes after the first flurry of feathers, they were all settled in upper branches, and all facing the sun. Stillness settled over the land, and it seemed an almost-religious vigil. The sun lowered, and went below the horizon, but still the birds sat as if in meditation. Then, as dusk itself began to fade into blackness, and the warmth of the sun leaked away to be replaced by the cold whiteness of the now-risen moon, there was another airborne scurrying as the birds sought out roosting places for the night, lower down and deeper into the trees. After a handful of irate squabbles over choice places, followed by a few minutes of general gossip and chit-chat, the birds quieted, and it was night. Adam got up and headed for the bathhouse.

The 6 o'clock news, which they missed, told of two more small earthquakes, near Brawley and San Fernando, in Southern California. It did not tell about the "contingency plans" being mapped-out at Fort Irwin which included martial law, or about the decision in Menlo Park to recommend that the Governor issue at least a general warning, or about the Governor's political decision to issue no warning at all. The people at Fort Irwin had buried any responsibility they might have felt for the problem, and were glowing with their importance and the prospect of being among the handful of powerful people under a state of martial law. The people at Menlo Park believed that the public should be warned; the people at Sacramento and Fort Irwin were in full agreement that the public should be told as little as possible.

Shawn, Mary, Adam, Sam, Hank, Moon, and Loner were at peace, soaking in their 10-foot by 10-foot redwood tub. There were bay leaves floating on the surface, and a life-size rubber duck was being scudded back and forth. Because they were moving around in water, they didn't feel the very mild shifting of the earth as the small, curving arm of land connecting Bodega Head with the mainland sank beneath the water, taking with it 17 houses. It didn't sink far, and no lives were lost, but the 15 families who were home at the time learned something new about living on top of a fault zone. But Bodega Bay was miles away from the ridge where the family lived, and the subsidence was gentle. The family were discussing what to put in the garden this year, and whether or not to spend some of their small cash income on rabbits to add variety to their diet.

At 7 p.m. the scientists at Menlo Park agreed that there was a good chance of a large earthquake somewhere along the thousands of miles of the California fault system. They notified the Governor, and recommended (with a strong feeling of professional doom) that he begin evacuation of the major cities. It was now after dark, which would add an incalculable amount of chaos. The Governor asked how certain they were.

"The probability is statistically significant . . . present level of expertise in the field . . ."

"In plain English."

"Better than even odds."

The Governor broke the connection and called three unlisted numbers, one of which was answered at Fort Irwin by the President's representative from Washington.

At 7:30 p.m. the people at the four major dams at the top of the Central Valley received instructions to increase the lowering of the reservoir lakes according to a schedule which was read over the telephone to them. The person in charge at Shasta Dam answered that the new schedule would cause flooding along the Sacramento River, and was told, "This is a direct order, with backing all the way to the Governor's office—and beyond. Adequate measures are being taken, but that is not your concern."

Hank and Moon were in their cabin getting dressed for the cold, damp evening, after returning from the bathhouse.

"I'm scared, Hank."

"What's the matter?"

"I'm afraid there's going to be an earthquake."

"Don't worry. Even if there was an earthquake, I wouldn't let anything happen to you. You just stick close to Hank, and everything'll be O.K."

Hank walked over, put his arms around Moon, and gave her a bear-hug. Then, sliding his hands down her back, he gave her soft, round bottom a reassuring squeeze.

"You know," he said stepping back and looking at her, "when your body is all red like that from the cold, it's almost as beautiful as mine. Let's get up to the house where the fire's going, before you turn blue."

The new schedule went into effect at all four dams before 8 o'clock, and the Feather and American rivers began to rise and to dump their increasing volumes into the already-rising Sacramento River. Evacuation of the flood plains along all three of the rivers began even as the calls were being made to the dams. The Sacramento Weir was thrown open, and as much water as possible was diverted through the old Ship Channel and the Yolo Bypass, and away from Sacramento. San Francisco Bay Area politicians were notified.

The family were happily clustered in front of the fireplace in the main house by 8 p.m. Shawn turned on the TV to check the news, leaving the sound off until there was something worth listening to. When the face on the screen looked interesting, Sam reached up and turned on the sound. The newsactor was recounting the earlier earthquakes: ". . . there was a 3.5 shock near San Luis Obispo in Central California. The most recent quakes were reported near Tahoe City and, for the second time today, Eureka. The nuclear power plant just south of Eureka is being shut down, apparently over the strong protest of its owner, Pacific Gas and Electric. Strictly as a precautionary measure, the levels of Clair Engle (Trinity), Shasta, Oroville, and Folsom lakes are being lowered. This may cause minor flooding along the Sacramento, Feather, and American rivers. We have been informed by the Governor's office in Sacramento that there is absolutely no danger to persons or property. The appropriate authorities have the situation well in hand."

Hank came into the living room carrying a jug of wine. While those who wanted some were helping themselves, he filled the enormous hookah which Adam had made from a 5-gallon bottled-water jar. It looked like a squid with its tubular body and its twelve smoking tubes, five of which were clamped off with alligator clips. Mary threw a couple of pine logs on the fire, and they all settled down on pillows in front of it. Along with the sounds of the fire they heard another sound, like loud surf or a distant jet airplane. The noise grew louder, drowning out the sound from the fireplace, until it sounded like a train going past the house.

"Everybody outside!" screamed Loner. "It's an earthquake!"

The pandemonium of the next few seconds was replaced with an empty room, which is well. They had almost made it to the garden when the first shock hit, and the old house settled slowly, but not quietly, down into itself.

For the first and last time in its short life, ARIES saw a change in the distance between Goldstone and Pasadena. Across a distance so vast that it takes light a billion years to cross it, ARIES noted the 30-foot increase in the distance between its eyes, as Pasadena moved northwest away from Goldstone. The people at Fort Irwin noticed it too, and forgot forever their worries of responsibility and their dreams of power. The entire Los Angeles megalopolis, including Pasadena, was a monumental pile of rubble. In Sacramento, the Governor's indecision was resolved.

The nuclear reactor just south of Eureka did not go critical and become a thermonuclear bomb. The reinforced concrete building housing the reactor, along with the rest of the installation, simply fractured and was shaken into fragments. The waters along the coast rapidly receded, leaving clams, mussels, sea anemones, crabs, and other shallow-water life stranded. They did not die from exposure to the air, though, for the water soon returned—in a 40-foot wave. The wave came thundering up the coastal incline with all the power of aroused nature, carrying the debris of the nuclear reactor with it as it swept inland as far as the coastal bluffs, where it crashed against this immovable object and hurled itself into the air, expending the last of its outward energy. Like a pendulum after reaching one end of its swing, the water picked up speed and force as it returned. Along with the trees and people and topsoil, it carried the treasures which had been held within the heart of the nuclear reactor and its storage area: a year's production, or about 6 million grams, of Plutonium-239, of which 1/100th of a gram is fatal to an animal the size of a human being; Iodine-129, which will remain lethal for tens of millions of years; Cesium-137; Strontium-90. The wave, and all of its many passengers, rushed back off the coast to join the south-flowing Japan Current along the North American shore, and then on out into the heart of the Pacific. The Japan Current, once carrying life and the food for life, became a river of active death, sucking the life from every living thing it came near.

The family were being tossed around on the cold, wet earth of the garden, where they had scrambled between the first and second shocks. The main house was a ruin, the two-storied barn had collapsed, and the water-storage tank had ruptured. The gas and electric lines were snapped in several places, but nobody was about to try to reach the shut-offs. The farm animals were loose, and those which weren't running in panic were trying to sink into the ground. Some chickens were hysterically clinging to their roosts in the trees, but most had already been shaken out, and were being hysterical on the ground. The hogs were squealing, and wallowing as deep into the mud as they could. Smoke started in the corner of the house where the fireplace had been, and was soon joined by flames. The shaking subsided, struck again with even greater force, subsided. All was quiet now except for the animals and the sounds of things settling down. The settling noises quieted to an occasional crack of breaking wood, and the fire in the jumble that had been the main house grew louder.

"I think it's stopped," Sam said. "I'll try to get the animals rounded up before they disappear."

"I'll take the electricity," Hank said.

"Two people had better take the gas and electricity," said Shawn, "just to be safe. I'll come with you."

"I'll get the water," Adam said.

"There's nothing we can do about the main house," Mary said, "and everything else can wait. Come on Loner, Moon—let's give Sam a hand with the animals."

The Melones-Hoadley fault area running from Oroville through Redding let loose with a jolt that was felt throughout the vast flatness of the northern Central Valley. The dams at Clair Engle, Shasta, Oroville, and Folsom lakes gave up within minutes of one another. Once Trinity Dam was gone, Lake Clair Engle smashed through Lewiston and Whiskeytown dams as if they were made of paper, adding their lakes to its own. They joined the waters of Lake Shasta in the Sacramento River just south of where Keswick Dam had been, and just exactly where Redding had been. Lake Oroville and half-a-dozen other man-made lakes on the east side of the Valley dumped into the Feather River, and joined the Sacramento River at Verona, to advance on Sacramento as a massive wall of water. Folsom Lake rushed into the American River, which joins the Sacramento River at Sacramento. When the waters had passed the state capital, there was nothing but a vast plain of mud, as far as the eye could see.

The frantic time was over. Moon was in shock, and Hank was holding her in his lap and rocking, talking quietly in her ear. Loner went off to the cabins to get blankets, and a first-aid kit to tend the minor injuries the family had received. Sam was still calming the animals, who were almost as important to him as the human members of the family. Adam was in the garage after moving the vehicles outside, making sure that if there were any more shocks, there would be no fire. Mary had a small fire going in the garden, and was making coffee and soup. Shawn was doing what only Shawn could do. He was the rock to which the rest of the family clung for stability; he was the nucleus which kept the electrons from spinning off in all directions. He sat in the garden, externally quiet, calm, and unexcited, giving the others the security they needed to go and do what they felt they should. His was the hardest task of all.

The leading wave of the flood rushed toward the safety of the sea. In its reckless haste it spread wide across the delta and tidelands between the place where Sacramento had been, and San Francisco Bay. It reared up as it hit the narrows of Carquinez Strait, and cascaded over into the Bay, scouring San Rafael and Richmond off the shores. It banked off the west side of the Bay taking out half of San Francisco, and all of San Mateo, Redwood City, and Palo Alto. It momentarily extended the south end of the Bay to include most of San Jose, the oldest town in California. On its back-sweep it took Fremont, Hayward, Alameda, and Oakland as far east as the hills, and then Tiburon, Sausalito, and the rest of San Francisco as it hurled itself out through the Golden Gate.

For the rest of the world, the tale is told of destruction by flood first, and by fire the next time. San Francisco, always known for its stubborn independence, did it exactly the opposite way.

The family were huddled around the campfire with their shoulders touching. They needed the security of the family, and it was there.

"Loner?" Shawn said softly. "Do you know if it's over?"

Loner didn't answer right away, but finally said, "There will be more shocks, but I think the worst is over." She paused for a long time, and then shakily continued. "All the theories come from past experience, and since people started writing it down, nothing like this has happened. There were so many quakes in so many different places. It's so big. I just don't know. I don't know," and for the first time anyone in the family had seen, Loner was crying.

Shawn let her cry for a while, and then moved over to her and put his arm around her shoulders, and squeezed gently. "Loner—relax. It's O.K. We're all alive, and we're all safe. It's alright if you don't know everything. It makes you easier to love." He gave her another squeeze, and then sat quietly with his arm around her. She cried more deeply, but there was joy mixed with the dread and pain. A few minutes later Loner came out the other side of her Change, and the first thing she said was, "Shawn—thank you." The earth trembled slightly, and everyone froze. It passed quickly. Loner said, "O.K., here's what I think is going to happen. The Big One has hit, and we're going to be getting after-shocks for the next several days or weeks—or maybe even months. There may be some big ones in the next few days, but probably not as big as the one that killed the house. We're going to have to camp out for awhile, though. I sure wish I had a drink." Shawn grinned, reached into a pocket of his bear-like coat, and pulled out his bottle of Irish whiskey.

The earth had been awakened by the early-morning nuclear blast, had groaned and stretched, and was gradually settling back to rest. There was no sleep for people this night, as several more strong shocks punctuated the almost-constant low grumbling. The Los Angeles Basin had subsided, and was under more than 100 feet of salt water—the ocean now came in as far as the San Gabriel and San Bernardino mountains. Sacramento had been flushed down the river. The San Francisco Bay Area—caught between the San Andreas and the Hayward faults, and then hit by the greatest flood in California's history—was no more. No major city had survived. Fires raged out of control throughout the state.

The family sat quietly in the garden watching the eastern horizon as it shaded from black into pearl-gray. A light breeze blew toward the east as the gray filled with scarlet and deep orange. A point of molten gold, and then as the sun rose from behind Sonoma Mountain, light and warmth. Dawn, on the first day of Spring.

L.A.P. Moore's short stories and articles are published in the USA, Canada and Australia. He is a member of the National Writers Club and "a native of Earth."

"You are becoming too independent and I will not have it."

Dona Lula and the Quetzal

BY YURI KOSSATCH

A pious beauty . . . but not to all.

I know, Señores, that the appearance of a Quetzal foreshadows misfortune. You know, do you not, what a Quetzal is? This is a bird rarely seen in our part of the country, for it dislikes the hubbub surrounding a village, and lives in the solitude of the jungle. You will always recognize the Quetzal by its purple feathered breast and its green wings. Our Quetzal, Señores, is like the eagle, a majestic bird. Do not, in any case be misled by its deceptive beauty. Keep in mind, that should you see this bird, perhaps in your garden, expect disaster. Only the consecration of a candle to San Juan Zacatapec can protect you.

Didn't I tell all this to Dona Lula, when that ominous bird lit into a treetop here in this yard? It flew down, sat in the anemone for a while and then flew off. Though everyone in the household, and even our neighbors in Totonicapan said that misfortune would visit the house of Dona Lula, she laughed this off as Indian superstition. None of us dared to contradict this cultured and educated lady, this the richest widow in our province, Dona Lula Caterina Alvarez de las Asturias Nava. At once beautiful and pious, Dona Lula was descended from a proud and ancient family, her ancestors having come here with Alvarado.

When our chickens died off, I reminded Dona Lula of the bad omen and begged her to be reasonable and to seek the protection of the Saint. Shortly thereafter a small ranch-house was destroyed by the fire. From managing her own estates she had grown accustomed to deal with a certain amount of trouble, for instance with her chicleros, so she gave little thought to greater calamities that might follow and even less would she consider the past misfortune as an admonition. Each year from May to November she employed Quechi tribesmen to cut sapota in the jungle near the ruins of Narano, and, also on her cacao plantation near Totonicapan. She was a sharp one and knew how to handle these Indians. They are like God's creatures. They need so little, just a handful of beans and their tortillas. How they honored and liked her, their mistress! Then again, who didn't like her, the Señora. Indeed it was something to see her at church in Totonicapan, or our fiesta honoring San Cristobal. She would appear like some splendid bird, walking in her high heeled shoes, her gowns which were made for her in the Capitol City after the newest French models, and her hair impaled by an ornate comb. All the best gentlemen, the richest fincleros, formed her retinue. Little girls presented her with flowers, and the padres more than willingly offered her their blessings.

Our Dona Lula was both courageous and self reliant. You might find it hard to believe, but three times a year she would herself drive a team in order to visit a holy place, and more frequently in order to go to Santa Cruz Queche, or to visit the distant city of Salama, not to mention going to Totonicapan, never accompanied by anyone other than a youngster. Though there is many a rich man in Totonicapan who would have willingly taken her any place in the country by car, she didn't like autos. When she approached a shrine she would hand over the reins and come up to the holy place barefoot. That is how pious she was.

It is true that evil tongues maintained that she made these trips not just to pray before the shrines of the San Domingo Xenaxcos or San Miguel de Tucuru. Often chattering gossips said that she preferred young confessors who had just left their seminaries and had not yet learned to impose heavy penances on erring widows. They said that it was her habit, after confession and absolution to find some young and handsome pilgrim with whom to do penance. Obviously she had suitors, if only those who coveted her beauty, her wealth or both. But that she should have entertained these unknown pilgrims I cannot believe. I will not say a bad word against her, except perhaps once in sorrow for her shortsightedness. The dreadful promise held out by that bird of ill omen far surpassed anything like a chicken plague or any other such trouble.

On the eve of the fiesta of the Holy Trinity, many guests had come to pass the holiday with Dona Lula. As is our custom, an altar resplendent with candles had been erected in the salon to the honor of the Holy Virgin, where day and night a large number of candles burned. As it happened, one of these candles was stolen. I tell you none but Dona Lula would have realized this. Nothing ever escaped her sharp eyes. No corner was too far or too dark to remain unknown to her. Nobody ever fooled her in anything. Naturally this missing candle caused us great shame before everyone. We were shamed before Padre Alvarengo, the guests, and most of all before the Holy Virgin, whose candle this was. Dona Lula assembled all her domestics and her Indians, the Maxenos and Queche. "Who stole the Virgin's candle?" she asked. Señores, could you but have seen the fire in her eyes. Dona Lula loved order and she could not tolerate this slight done to the Holy Virgin. Dona Lula was a good woman but when she had right behind her it was best not to cross her. Apart from this, Señores, what good Christian could tolerate so heinous a deed?

"If the guilty one is not found immediately," she swore at the Indians, "then with or without the police, I'll find the thief if it's the last thing that I do. You are becoming too independent and I will not have it. And now, this worst kind of miscreance, thievery . . ."

Padre Alvarengo tried to calm her by telling her that candles were always stolen from him, and in any event the candle was of no great value. As to its purpose, he could consecrate another and the Virgin

149

would be no worse off. "To me," said Dona Lula, "it is the same whether it cost thousands or nothing. This is a matter of principle. Padre, I do not expect either decency or gratitude from my Indians, only order. If you do not train a dog properly he will be worse than useless. What am I to do with these dogs, if not to teach them order and respect for the Holy Virgin?"

The incident was further discussed and considered, but the Indians did not yield up the thief, for in truth they did not know that the candle had been taken by a little boy, who upon hearing of the search for the one who had taken the candle fled into the jungle. Two days later he was found and brought before Dona Lula. This frightened Chichi trembled in his fear as if with ague, just whispering one thing over and over: "I wanted a candle for San Juan del Obispo. I wanted the candle for San Juan del Obispo . . ."

"You were to honor the Holy Virgin, and not San Juan del Obispo, you stupid monkey!. . ." No one had ever seen Dona Lula in such a fury. "What is your San Juan to me, idiot? Why did you take the Virgin's candle?"

"I wanted the candle for San Juan del Obispo . . . I wanted the candle for San Juan . . ."

Dona Lula struck him right across his face, and then gave an order to see to it that this "Chichi" received twenty-five lashes from the whip. The conversation among the guests in the salon turned to Dona Lula. Padre Alvarengo himself observed that Dona Lula was blessed with more than womanly shrewdness not to expect gratitude from the Indians. He was told of the Indians often praying before their saints for freedom from the white señores who had long ago taken up this land and made them work, to be taken away to hell from this country. These Indians do not deserve anything more than the whip.

Others observed that the Indians had only one interest, which was not to work, and should any money come their way to drink aguardiente. There is, said one neighboring finclero, no reason to think that they ever will be, even if literate, any better. To the contrary, in that event they would probably be dangerous.

Thus the talk went on in its customary ways and San Juan del Obispo did not help his "Chichi," for shortly after the whipping the youngster took ill and died. I am, Señores, of the opinion that he died of dysentery, which is common enough among the Indians. Certainly this "Chichi" did not warrant much more consideration. In any event there are more children among the Indians than they can feed, hence the thievery.

As you know, Señores, ten days ago the builders came to this section to make the big road which is to run the length of our country. Their work left us for a few days with no way to Totonicapan except the paths through the jungle. Why just then did Dona Lula decide to go to Totonicapan? I cannot say. Some will tell you that she had a suitor awaiting her there, with whom she was going to go to Santa Cruz Queche. This I do not believe. If indeed there was this caballero, then God be with him, for Dona Lula never reached Santa Cruz, nor did she ever get to Totonicapan.

Afterwards, a little girl who had accompanied Dona Lula told us what had happenned. Following a road she knew very well, Dona Lula had driven some way into the jungle when three armed Indians stepped out of the roadside bush. They seized the horses' bridles, stopping them and ordered Dona Lula to get down from the rig. As was her habit Dona Lula wore high heeled shoes and so was able to walk only with considerable difficulty through the jungle undergrowth. She swore at the Indians and called upon all the Saints and even Holy Maria for help. This of course was to no avail and Dona Lula was forced to go into the jungle following the three Naxenos. The little girl remained in the rig as ordered and nothing happened to her. Later this fact made some suspect that she was somehow connected with these Indians. But that is doubtful for that little goose was frightened half to death and knew nothing. Finally when the horses were tired of standing there and impatient at the insect bites they turned and came home rig and all.

Immediately, parties went out with dogs and lights to search for Dona Lula. The fincleros were ready to shoot down any Indians like rabbits. Fortunately they had all hidden in their villages. On the second day of the search, deep in the jungle, Dona Lula was found. If you know where the redwood is being cut, Señores, you will know the place. She was found, forgive me, stark naked, tied to or rather hanging from a tree, the same way her overseers in the forest near

Narano would leave an unruly or lazy chiclero for a day or so. I do not know whether she was hanging there a long time or not . . . I do know that not very much of our pretty Dona Lula was found there, only what the beasts and insects of the jungle left.

Señores she was given a noble funeral. You should have seen how the people wept for her, especially the neighboring pretenders for having let much properties slip through their fingers. All her estates, plantations and forests with their chicleros passed into the hands of her younger sister who is married to an officer of police in Antigua.

So did the Quetzal prophecy come to pass, and such was the fate of our beautiful pious Dona Lula. She was a mother to the Indians and an example to us. Señores, never expect gratitude or fidelity from the Indians. I am blaming Dona Lula for she did not remember her duty to San Juan Zacatapec. He might have kept her from the evil of the Quetzal. But she did not hold San Juan Zacatapec in the highest regard.

Born in 1909 in Kiev, Yuri Kossatch's literary activity dates from 1927 in Lviv where his short stories, poems, novels and essays were first published in Western Ukrainian periodicals. He has received numerous literary prizes. An authority on Ukrainian literature, his work has been translated into English, Polish, French, German, Russian and Portuguese. The story was translated by his son, George Kossatch, Jr.

"He is not going to live in the clouds,
but on the ground, among people."

A Trip Into Life

BY MEŠA SELIMOVIĆ

A young witness to life's crudities.

WHEN I asked my father for permission to take a trip with the coachmen, I was both frightened and apprehensive. The idea seemed to me to be too free, somehow incomprehensible, almost daring; it was not an everyday occurrence but almost an adventure in the face of which I felt sweet trepidation. And I was afraid, too, that he would ask me who put me up to this. I didn't know if I would dare to lie because his blue, blazing eyes, with their shaggy eaves of eyebrows, were terrifying. You couldn't hide anything from them. And I didn't want to betray my friend, the young coachman, Asim, who had invited me to join him on the trip. He had asked me with enthusiasm: "You'll see," he told me, "you'll see how beautiful it is!" He was interesting and dear. He used to tell me exciting stories about girls, about people, about strange trips through the night, about lonely inns along the roads. There was no fear in his words. He never hesitated as he spoke of all these things, not whitewashing them or sneering or winking. He was innocent. He spoke to me about life in an unusual way; he made it sound jovial and victorious. Nobody knew about this but us because we kept to ourselves, preferring to talk in the hay-filled attic of the long barn, especially when the rain was falling, striking the shingles above us. Wide-open as a flower, I listened to him, being afraid to question or to say even one word, for fear of breaking the hum of this distant, unknown life which intoxicated me.

And now it was necessary for me to go into the world. This, here, wasn't the world. This was the house, familiar from top to bottom, the large yard and garden in whose shadows I used to dream about that life beyond my vision, the dusty books which were filling me with dangerous excitement, and a desire for wide-open spaces, the long barns with the most unpleasant odors of leather harnesses and horse dung, and the strange stories of the coachmen in the evening at sunset, under the mulberry tree; everything was close, dear, still a little annoying because nothing threatened me with the unexpected. And somewhere out there was the world and life—exciting, full of adventures, strange encounters, heroism—complicated but majestic as a revolving circle of great events. I didn't know their nature and for that very reason, they attracted me. I was excited.

Meanwhile, everything was resolved very simply. My father consented. He was healthy, tough, invulnerable and felt that everyone else should be the same way. Especially his children. Therefore, he didn't sense any of my anxieties. I only heard him telling my mother (I didn't hear my mother's voice because she expressed all her qualms quietly): "Let him go, let him see. He is not going to live in the clouds, but on the ground, among people."

So, early in the morning, when I climbed aboard the coach, still sleepy, I found a blanket and food, placed there by unknown hands. In the darkness, I could make out that Alma, our trotter, was harnessed to the light coach with springs, I saw Asim tightening the harnesses, I heard the voice of old Kreho, his father, as he shouted orders, and I knew that he would travel with us, too. I was awake when the ten loaded carts started moving, I heard the sharp, bronze sounds from the front of the caravan, and then I fell asleep on the soft pile of hay.

I was awakened by the hot summer sun. It was baking the dusty road, painted white, in front of us and behind us. It continued to burn down on us. This was the region I knew: the small settlement, the church with its high spire, and the immense oak tree next to it. And then—the unknown. And then—goodbye! I turned back, searching for the church spire and the immense oak tree, that limit of my world. Goodbye!

The alien world was empty: the unbearably white road which smarted the eyes, the gloomy houses alongside the road or on the slopes, the silent, dark forests in the distance, the old inns, moldy and foreboding, where we sometimes stopped, and sadness began to overtake me. I don't know why. I was losing the feeling of the morning that nothing essential had changed, that one part of the house was traveling with me, that with these familiar coaches and horses, with these ten or so men whom I knew, a part of my sky traveled with us, that in all this unknown we brought something of ours, as if we had gained the right of extraterritoriality in each place where we found ourselves. I began to feel the alien world and I couldn't check the storm of sorrow. The bells on the first horses were no longer ringing; they had served as a buffer for my anxiety. And these people I knew were now different than the ones I had known before. They were silent and gloomier than usual. Asim moved the whip slowly as though he were chasing flies from Alma and he kept silent. And his father, old Kreho, was also silent. Old Kreho wasn't old, they just called him that. He wasn't even fifty. His eyes were flashing, fiery, insatiable, and his motions swift and restless. It was as if something constantly flared up within him, some constant motion that never allowed his eyes, his hands, or his tongue to be at peace. Yet even he was quiet. At certain inns and storehouses he would stop and talk about things with people I didn't know, explaining, arguing, bargaining and leaving empty sacks. These were grain-collection stations where we would collect the loaded sacks on our return. Then he would sit in the coach again, silent. He had tried to talk but he didn't succeed. He couldn't warm up to the idea of telling a story to a twelve-year old child. And to his son he paid no attention at all. He probably never talked to him! And when he was bored with the silence, he stepped down from the coach and spoke to Adjul. I knew that alongside Adjul's wide seat of hay, under which there was always a bottle of slivovic, one of the greatest conversations, chuckfull of adventures, would take place; full of shrewd observations, of the fresh sensations of people who don't like abstractions and who accept everything through their senses. I liked those conversations that scared me.

I knew that Asim would start talking to me once Kreho left. And I knew about whom. About Marica. Marica was in Kalesija, where we were to spend the night, and, for that reason he mentioned Kalesija often. He was eighteen years old, the same as Marica. He spoke of love in scant words but to me the scarcity did not take away from the enthusiasm, maybe because there was so much sincerity in his voice. He asked me if I knew what love was. I didn't know; I guessed but I didn't know. Only I was ashamed to admit that. He looked at the hills in front of us: only that one, then that one, and one more, and then Kalesija. And Marica. A transformation came over Asim when he talked about her. He became different. His lips trembled strangely, his voice was more subdued and hoarse, his gray eyes grew softer. I began to look forward to Kalesija and Marica and love.

Darkness came as a surprise. It was as though night were falling for the first time at the beginning of the world and things became what they were not or what we thought they were not. The occurrence called out for sorrow. Yesterday, and before that, it was different, more simple. Now it was darkness, a burden, a compression into one's self, sight which didn't see. Near and far were the same. Nothingness. And fear. The lit kerosene lamps that hung at the end of each coach in front of us swung helplessly. That yellow swinging made us restless, never really lighting anything, not cheering us, yet not ceasing until it went out. Everything around me was as tired as I was: the horses' neighing, the stars' flickering, the coachmen's voices. Those voices were now different, having changed from day to night into muffled, deep, excited tones. They sounded especially strange when the coaches stopped next to the water trough to water the horses. At once everything stopped living because there was no movement; the swinging of the lamps stopped, the night stormed in ominously. Only the voices and hummings were heard. Bad luck? You didn't question. You knew that it wasn't but, in a way, it was, for something could happen even if it didn't. For everything was a contradiction. The crickets along the road, bordered by yellow flowers with yawning mouths, chirped in a strange manner. That chirping had a yellow smell, but how could chirping have a smell? And how could the smell be yellow? With those confused thoughts, I fell asleep.

Asim's voice woke me up: "Kalesija."

That sounded cheerful and delightful. As if he had announced: happiness! He repeated it again: "Kalesija!" He was convincing himself and the world that he was within reach of his desires, that the realization of his dreams would begin.

On the left side of the road, a few lights flickered at the window in an inn, with large black eaves overhanging. Signaling with the kerosene lamps, the coachmen drove in, one by one, over the small wooden bridge and parked their coaches under the inn's eaves. They unharnessed the horses, dried them off with bundles of hay, and went at once into the inn. After the horses had cooled off, they returned to give them water and oats; they never forgot that. Kreho gave orders which seemed unnecessary, left Žiga to guard the coach, and then approached us.

"We'll spend the night here," he said. I knew that. I knew even more than he did. "There are rooms with beds in the inn but (he turned to me) I think it's better for you to sleep in the coach. There are all kinds of vermin inside. You're not afraid?"

I was afraid of vermin and the night; more of the night than of vermin. But I didn't say anything. For a long time I hid what I was thinking from others.

In the large ground-floor room of the old inn, we found only a few people. At first I didn't take notice of much due to bashfulness more than to the tobacco smoke and poor lighting, because Kreho was proudly introducing me to the owner of the inn and to the others who were there. I was confused by a female hand which caressed my face. I retreated into myself. I knew that she was Marica. I didn't see her face, I saw the edge of her waving polka-dot dress and shoes. Nothing else. And I was certain that it was she. Asim was sitting next to me, along the wall. When he looked up, I saw that he was flushed and excited. After the fog of my shyness was dispersed, I saw things around me more clearly. There were about five or six tables, rough-hewn, without tablecloths. Next to us sat two gendarmes, a chubby peasant, and a young man with ruddy complexion and reddish hair, wearing city clothes. I didn't find out who he was or why he was there. He looked like a traveling salesman. The owner of the inn was thin, dirty, stooped, constantly smiling, taciturn but appearing as if he were participating in every conversation by his smile, by listening, with gestures, with everything except words. He was sitting down and he gave orders to Marica with his eyes, prodding her, reproaching her, pacifying her. His eyes had feet and wings. They were running and flying everywhere, unremittingly and relentlessly, and everything in him was lazy and motionless except his eyes.

When Marica brought me some milk, Asim beckoned to her to come out. She lowered her eyelashes and smiled. Did she agree? Then she brought drinks to the rest. The traveling salesman was fondling his sideburns, casting his eyes on her with the most seductive look he could manage. He asked her if she had liquor. There was no liquor. Too bad, he said, and he blew into her face cigarette smoke which he held at the edge of his thin mouth. The gendarmes, already drunk, reached out their leaden hands but she evaded them and smiled. She looked at us and we looked at her. The fire did not go out in Asim's eyes. I was impressed with his enthusiasm and I hated all these people as much as he did.

I didn't get a definite picture of her, not even a single line or expression; I only knew that she was lively, full of motion, slim, and beautiful. She was beautiful not from what I saw but from what I had learned about her a long time ago. Beautiful. No, she was more than that. She was love. Asim sat nailed to the wall, which had been peeled by many backs that had rested here, and he absorbed her insatiably into himself, bridging the gap between them with his eyes and, in return, her smiles came across that gap, licking his face like flames which burned him and made him blush. Did Kreho notice those kisses of the eyes? I didn't know but he interrupted them rudely and suddenly, telling us that it was time to go to bed. To bed? He didn't know anything. Or maybe he did.

We left. Asim leaned his elbows on the rungs of the coach. "You lay down," he said.

"And you?"

"I can't . . . isn't she beautiful?"

"Yes."

"She's beautiful. And I love her." And then he moaned: "If she doesn't come out, I'll die."

He was eighteen years old and I twelve. I didn't understand many things but I truly thought that he would really die. I got scared, I felt sorry for him, but I wasn't able to tell him anything.

"You sleep," he told me. "I'll be here."

He moved from under the shadows of the eaves into the moonlit yard and approached the window where, concealing himself, he looked into the room we had just left. Inside the noise was growing like a parrot's chatter. There were more and more voices and they were stronger; slivovic gave them the right and the strength. They're stronger, they're crazier, and less and less coherent. The screaming and clatter began to choke me. Sometimes, just for a moment, I caught distinct words but they soon died out and the confusion remained, like men screaming in animal cages. I knew the majority of them in that room and now I wouldn't go near them. What had awakened in them? And who were they now? I was afraid of them and I trembled for fear that they would cut one another's throats. The din and roar implanted the idea of impending catastrophe in me; something would happen, had happened already because the people no longer existed, only madness. If it spilled over from the inn, it would erase everything in its path: the eaves and the horses and the whole world, and only desolateness and panic would remain, the same panic that overtook me and everything around me.

From time to time, they came out of the inn, into the yard, to relieve themselves. One staggered toward the horses who were munching barley. He grunted at them and then he came to my coach and his drunken, sour, whiskey-bathed hand stumbled upon me. I became paralyzed for I thought he was reaching for my neck, to squeeze my throat with his hard, calloused thumb, or for my eyes, to dig them out with his black nails. Instead, the hand pulled the blanket over my shoulders unsteadily and touched my hair and then he sneaked out of the coach like a lazy snake. I was not at ease until the reeling figure went back into the inn. I didn't know them. Yesterday I knew them.

Each time somebody came out of the inn, Asim hid in the darkness, waiting his chance to return to the window and stare into the room. He was waiting for Marica. At last she came out. Her dress shone like silver in the moonlight. She went to him at once, and he to her, as though they were magnets. They hid in the shadows and started to whisper. Later, Asim disclosed to me everything I didn't see. Truly sobbing, he told me the story and all the voids I filled in myself, certainly not then, but much later. He didn't invent the words of love he spoke to her there in the darkness behind the inn, on that pile of dung. Other people had invented them long before he. But it was the same as if he had created them for they were born from him for the first time, and those newly-born words, reeking with inexperience and incoherence, acquired meaning from the conviction and love which complemented everything they weren't. Suddenly, Marica started to cry. She was crying for herself; another's words provoke one's own joys and sorrows. He was hurt by her tears and he tried to dry them up with implorings, babblings, and proposals. One proposal, crazy, dangerous, above his power (which only female tears could evoke) was to take her with him, in his coach, no matter where, then to return before dawn when everyone would still be drunk, or have left, or have died; it was all the same to him. She accepted that proposal at once except that she modified it: he should take her, not just anywhere, but to Zvornik and she would not come back at dawn, for she did not want to come back at all. A long time in the making, this decision reached maturity that night. The moldy old inn next to the road and dead Kalesija had become unbearable for her. She had grown tired of the innkeeper's eyes warning, controlling, pushing, and reproaching her. In front of her stood the dream of a life other than this one in Kalesija; it was all to become reality that night. Still waiting for her in the inn were the thirsty drunkards with their wooden faces while this foolhardy youth, with his tender words, opened all the faucets of her heart. Now only sorrow was pouring out of him, for maybe she longed for Zvornik because she loved someone there, but maybe she only wished to escape from Kalesija.

The traveling salesman came out the door and sniffed the moonlight. "Honey, where are you?" he called, tenderly.

From the open window, the innkeeper, not able to see her, yelled into the night: "Marica! Marica!"

She went back in to quiet them down.

Asim came back to the coach and, with jumbled speech, he explained to me that he was going to Zvornik, that he would be back at dawn, and that I ought to move into another coach and not say anything to anyone. In vain, I pointed out the dangers to him. He knew about them but he hoped that nobody would find out. And as for the idea that his father would find out, he dismissed it with a wave of the hand. I moved into another coach. Asim harnessed Alma and quietly, making as little noise as possible, drove the coach out on to the road. Then one moment went by, two, five, the whole of eternity, until Marica came out with a small bag in her hand. She ran through the yard and they got lost in the night. All that could be heard was the rolling of the wheels and the striking of the horses' hooves on the hard road. Trembling, I wished luck to those who were longing for it. I heard my scared heart in the silence, which reigned over the road as a harbinger. The voices from the inn expressed anxiety; Marica wasn't there. One of the gendarmes came out into the yard, staggering and looking for her, talking to himself. He could barely walk but he was looking for her. The innkeeper came out and ordered into the night: "Marica!" He was looking for her, too, and, not finding her, he became scared. "Marica! Marica!"

That useless calling stuck to my brain. I was afraid, I shivered. Only I knew where Marica was. But they would find out too. What would happen? I suffered from the irrational feeling that I was guilty, that I was involved in everything, and would pay the price for it. We kidnapped Marica. More of them were in the yard, their voices excited and dangerous. They ran around like a reconnaissance party, like hound dogs. The former panic overtook me again. Probably because it was night and I was all alone. Maybe because the crickets chirped so excitedly and the nearby meadow smelled so heavy. I didn't know why. And the moonlight was frightening; the moonlight with shadows in which all the fears of a twelve-year-old lay. But my worst fear came from the people; they were searching and searching in vain. As they got nearer, Kreho saw that there was no coach and no Alma.

"Where did they go?" Kreho asked me.

I didn't dare lie. I showed him only the direction but that was sufficient for him. Without saying anything, he approached one of the two horses which we had brought with us on our trip, harnessed it, and, with agility, jumped on it and flew off into the night.

Žiga and I were sleeping in the same coach, he up on the sacks and I on the seat. Žiga woke up and asked, yawning: "What's that? What was that noise?"

By then the noise had quieted down so he had probably heard it in his sleep. I told him.

"What will happen?" I asked him.

"If he reaches him, he'll beat him up," he said. Then he yawned innocently and soon he was snoring again.

Would he reach him? He reached him. Asim was in no special hurry for he was prolonging the happiness that this chance gave him. It took him a long time to get up the courage to place his arm around Marica's waist but once he did, he forgot about Alma and let her trot along as she wished. Then he heard the galloping hooves behind him. If he had picked up the reins and hollered at Alma, he could have escaped easily. Alma was an excellent runner and it was hard to find her equal. But he didn't do anything. He took his hand away from Marica's waist and became petrified. He decided that if it was his father it wasn't worth running away. And it was his father. He overtook them, stood in front of Alma and shouted only: "Turn around!"

He unmounted, tied his horse up at the end of the coach, and sat with them.

"Hurry up!" he said, sullenly. "I exhausted the horse because of you." And nothing else. In silence, they reached Kalesija.

While Asim unharnessed Alma, Kreho waited next to the coach. Marica went inside the inn. When the mare was settled, Kreho picked up the whip, heavy and tightly woven, and started to beat his son with the heavier front section. He didn't scream, curse, or utter a sound in advance of such violence. He didn't say anything; it was not necessary. Kreho beat him calmly, in a business-like manner, and horribly. Every so often he warned him not to cover his head. "Take your hands away! Take your hands away!"

Asim stood straight, facing his father. He didn't cry or pull away. Only after certain blows which were probably harder than the others, a deep, muffled moan could be heard, which escaped him unwillingly. I was terrified; this cold execution of tyranny under the guise of a parent's right crushed me. The strikes were so horrible that I began to feel as if the blows struck me, that the red marks and bloody streaks were on my body. Yet even that wasn't the worst of it. The worst was the thought—really not the thought but the consternation—that, after this, life wasn't worth living. I don't know how long I felt this way or if I felt this way in regard to myself or life in general or only as it affected Asim, but I do know that, for a long time, I carried the bitterness of such a feeling in my heart.

Having satisfied himself and justice, Kreho threw the whip into the coach and said: "Dry up both horses with hay. They're sweaty. In an hour, let them drink some water." Then he turned around and went into the inn.

I went to Asim. He sniffled loudly, spitting blood, and carefully felt his forehead. He came out from the shadows into the moonlight and looked at his fingers.

"I have to wash up," he said. His face was bloody.

We went to the well. With the bucket tied to the hoisting apparatus, he pulled up water, washed himself, cleaned up his nose and mouth. He soaked a handkerchief and put in on his forehead.

"Does it hurt you?" I asked, foolishly, not to find out but to show my compassion.

"Yes, it hurts," he answered, simply. "Tomorrow it will be black and blue."

"Are you hurt?"

My questions were stupid. I sensed that but I spoke about what bothered me.

"I feel hurt because he brought me back. The bruises will go away."

Later he dried the backs of the sweaty horses with hay.

"Lay down in our coach," he told me.

"And you?"

"I'll wait. When everyone falls asleep, she'll come out."

"She" is Marica. He thought only of her. And he waited. He

163

leaned against a thick pillar of the eaves and waited. The screams came from the inn again. But now it was different than earlier because Marica's voice could be heard more and more, her laughter, her singing. Asim moved away from the pillar and listened carefully, so carefully, hoping that he was wrong, that he was imagining things. He wasn't wrong. Marica was going mad, seeking revenge against anyone and anything for the way things were and for what didn't happen this night, or the night before, or any night up to now in her life. It was hard for her and she grieved in her own way: she was making herself immune to grief, wishing to go through this period of awakened desires without the light of conscience, as through a tunnel whose exit would be the next day. And that day could bring anything, either salvation or no regrets. And either one would make it possible for life to continue, even if with wounds.

Asim went back to the window and saw Marica go into a dark corner; everything was already the same to her. He wanted to go inside and to beg them, to cry out: "People, leave her alone! Give her to me as a present for this night. I love her. Give her to me, let me hide her from you and from herself and from the entire world, to shield her, even though she is now immune. Because all this hurts me. For days and months I have been dreaming about her and I never imagined a night such as this. I never thought about you, I never thought that this night and you would be here. But only she and I. Let it be that way!"

But he didn't go in, he didn't implore. He stood next to the window and suffered unbearably. Nevertheless, he bore up for, as time passed by, he stood there and had enough strength to watch and listen to everything.

Time was passing. I lay in the coach, weary but unable to fall asleep. Feverish visions troubled me. It was only after Asim came and fell into the coach next to me, awakening me, that I realized I had been asleep. Asim was shaking from crying. He bit the thick end of the whip to smother the sobs which burst forth from him.

"What's wrong with you?" I asked him, frightened. "What's wrong with you?" I repeated, and he acted as if he couldn't answer.

"My father . . ."

He squeezed out that word, wrinkled, spat upon, salty from tears, bitter from indignation, and then he added others which explained to me his despair.

The next day we traveled without saying a word. It was sad. Asim, black and blue, with bloody trails on his face, which was swollen from not sleeping, looked with hatred at his father who, last night, spoiled all the dreams he had had for months about Marica. Kreho was tired and silent. He stared at the white road stretching out ahead of us.

And I was sad and empty, tired and unhappy. I felt sorry for people, yet I had had my fill of people. My father had said: "He ought to see everything. Because he is not going to live in the clouds, but on the ground, among people."

Maybe he was right.

But, for a long time after that, Asim didn't tell his serene, victorious tales of life nor did I wish to hear them.

Meša Selimović is a prize-winning Bosnian writer of short stories and novels. The story was translated by Rosario Glasnovic, now a New York teacher who was born in the Croatian town of Janjevo and attended the University of Zagreb.

Coming up in future issues of SSI

USA	**Paul Theroux** The Railcar to San Salvador
Uganda	**Peter Nazareth** The Confessor
New Zealand	**Witi Ihimaera** Gathering of the Whakapapa
Italy	**Brunella Gasperini** Summer by the Sea
Ireland	**T.G. Nestor** Incentives
Chile	**José Donoso** The Closed Door
Austria	**Alois Vogel** The Parable of the Tightrope Walker
Korea	**Sunwu Hwi** The Revelation
Turkey	**Aziz Nesin** The People Are Awakening
Pakistan	**Razia Fasih Ahmad** Saasta
England	**R. Hudson-Smith** Assemblée Générale
Wales	**John Brereton** Second to None
Peru	**Mario Vargas Llosa** On Sunday
USA	**John Updike** Here Come the Maples
Sri Lanka	**Suvimalee Gunaratna** The Bus Ride
France	**Françoise Sagan** The Sun Also Sets

And, for your reading pleasure, other intriguing,
insightful stories from all lands.

For readers who can't read...

Greek, Arabic, Chinese, Japanese, Dutch, Norwegian, Chukchi, Finnish, Hindi, Turkish, Urdu, Hebrew, Russian, Vietnamese, Portugese, etc., etc.

Short Story International takes you to all points of the compass, to anywhere in the world. There are intriguing stories waiting for you in future issues of SSI—stories that will involve you in corners of this world you've never seen . . . and in worlds outside of this one . . . with glimpses into the future as well as the past, revealing fascinating, universal truths that bypass differences in language and point up similarities in peoples.

Send in the coupon below and every other month SSI will take you on a world cruise via the best short stories being published throughout the world today—the best entertainment gleaned from the work of the great creative writers who are enhancing the oldest expression of the entertainment arts—the short story.